KALAYUG

Anurag Tripathi is an alumnus of the Indian School of Business with a course in Advanced Creative Writing from The University of Oxford, Department for Continuing Education. An erstwhile investment banker, his deal-making pursuits and entrepreneurial ventures have given him key insights into the working of corporate business houses. He lives in Paris along with his wife. Both are avid divers, who like travelling and exploring the world lesser known.

KALAYUG

Kalā, sixty-four performing arts
Kal Yug, Kali Yuga, 'Age of Kali', the 'Age of Downfall'

Anurag Tripathi

RUPA

Published by
Rupa Publications India Pvt. Ltd 2017
7/16, Ansari Road, Daryaganj
New Delhi 110002

Sales centres:
Allahabad Bengaluru Chennai
Hyderabad Jaipur Kathmandu
Kolkata Mumbai

ISBN: 978-81-291-4236-8

First impression 2017

10 9 8 7 6 5 4 3 2 1

To my wife, my life partner,
thank you for loving me like a child,
despite my idiosyncrasies.

Contents

Chapter 1

You Just Got Conned!

Jay had been stuck in the same place for the last twenty minutes, a block away from the hotel. He had never been happier in a traffic snarl. He hoped the serpentine queue of cars was a testimony to a renewed interest in art in India. He wasn't late but he wanted to be early so he made the sacrifice of getting out of his Mercedes S Class and emerging into the humidity of the Mumbai afternoon, making his way slowly to the entrance. As he approached the gilded gates, he realised that the snarl ahead was the result of a Bollywood star and a politician arriving simultaneously. In Mumbai, if Bollywood, cricket and politics came together, it was a given that the event would be a success even before it started. He knew that the cricket element was inside already. After all, he had given a pass to the biggest icon of the game himself. The afternoon just kept getting better and better.

He had been deluged by requests for passes. He had ignored most and politely declined others. The art industry had grown and maintained itself on the basis of exclusion, both cultural and financial. He hadn't become an insider to demolish the snobbishness of the art elite. He had actually been pleasantly surprised by the demand for passes, especially since the last four years had been very bad for business. The global financial meltdown in 2008 had hugely affected the art industry. Transactions had died almost completely, forcing many of the art galleries, which had mushroomed across the country over the past decade, to shut down.

In this particular case, it had helped that an internationally renowned auction house was organising the auction. The auction had been billed as the 'Re-emergence of the art industry in India'. The event had become the hottest topic of discussion within the incestuous social circles of Delhi and Mumbai. The usual scramble to utilise their networks and call in favours to ensure names on the invitation list had followed. Every such event was akin to a relegation in super division football. The stragglers were relegated while the top performers amongst the second rung were elevated. The constant flux kept everyone on their toes.

People who had received the invitation made sure that everyone knew it, while those who were still trying to get one spoke about non-existent prior commitments which would mysteriously disappear if they actually succeeded in cadging an invite. The auction house had already changed its venue to a larger banquet hall in the same hotel to meet the extra demand.

A socialite had told him a few days earlier that she hadn't seen such a mad rush for a social event since the wedding reception hosted by the Mittals at Versailles Palace in 2004, when steel baron, Lakshmi Mittal's daughter got married. Over a thousand guests had been flown in from across the world to attend the grand party. It had lasted over a week and was rumoured to have cost a staggering $60 million. The fortunate few who had been invited to the reception had 'carelessly' kept the invitation cards under glass tabletops in their living rooms where guests could see them.

When he finally reached the main reception area outside the banquet hall, he discerned a buzz of commotion and excitement. The crowd here could be divided into three categories. Those he knew, those who knew him and those who did not matter. He greeted everyone with the same warmth. He well remembered what a cold shoulder had felt like, back when he was new to the art scene, and he had no intention of making enemies tonight. He had enough of those anyway.

This was the kind of gathering that kept Page 3 alive and gave tabloids their raison d'etre. The women looked exquisite. His eyes fell on Patty, noticing that the bitch still looked attractive. She hadn't put on an ounce since the last time he had seen her without her clothes on. The material of her dress clung to her curves, accentuating her full figure. She was holding court like a queen. Despite the fact that she no longer wielded the same power in the art world, as the owner of two distinguished art galleries she was still a regular at such events.

He cursed silently when Patty caught him looking at her. She broke off her conversation and moved towards him. It had been a long time since they had spoken and he wasn't sure he wanted to break that streak.

'Hello, Mr Malhotra. Mustering up the courage to talk to me, are you?'

'Nope, just trying to figure out how much weight you have put on. Your dress makes it rather easy. Have you been sleeping with your physical trainer lately?'

'Oh ho, someone's surly today. Can't blame you though. Can't find a buyer for all the Navaratnas on sale tonight? You know I would love to help you out. But I guess I would rather have your pants taken off and let people see what didn't impress me.' She turned away abruptly.

He watched her walk back to her coterie of admirers. Normally, he would have tried to get in the last word, but not tonight. He knew he would have the last laugh eventually. Patty didn't know that he had managed to arrange buyers for five of the seven Navaratnas coming up for auction.

It had been a close call though. He had to strain every sinew to ensure they were picked up. He couldn't have done it if it hadn't been for his friend Biswas Mukherjee, the art expert. Biswas had spoken to a few museum curators on his behalf and convinced one of them to bid for four paintings. But what he really looked forward to seeing was the reaction in the room when he bid a record-breaking amount on behalf of Deepak Patel.

He had found him by sheer luck. Or actually, Deepak had found him. Whatever it was, the encounter was what had put him in such a good mood. The turnout at the auction and the preceding buzz had given him hope that the other two paintings would be picked up too.

People had begun lining up at the auction almost an

hour earlier to register themselves and receive their paddles. Paddles helped identify bidders by virtue of specific numbers that were designated to them by the auction house. However, not everyone required paddles to bid; a mere raising of hands was sufficient if you were known to the auction house. A smile appeared on Jay's face as he recalled the story of Rembrandt's portrait. At the Christie's auction at London in 1965, the legendary American collector Simon Norton wanted to bid secretly for the painting and left the following instructions with Peter Chance, Christie's auctioneer:

'If seated, I am bidding. If I stand up, I have stopped bidding. If I sit down again, I am not bidding unless I raise my finger. When I raise my finger, I am bidding until I stand up again. Then I have stopped bidding.'

Simon sat throughout the bidding, but confused the auctioneer Peter Chance by bidding aloud and then remaining silent. Chance became convinced that although seated, Simon had stopped bidding. When the bid rose to 740,000 sterling pounds, Simon remained seated and silent. Chance panicked and sold the Rembrandt to another investor. Simon immediately stood up and disputed the result, stating, 'I had never stopped bidding, read my instructions out to all those present in the auction room.' The auction was restarted after some delay and Simon eventually bought the painting for 798,000 sterling pounds.

But that was then. The days of simple auctions were over. Auctions today were complex, run by psychologists and masters of understanding, interpreting and manipulating consumer behaviour. From the invitation list to the seating arrangement, everything was done according to a master plan.

The invitation list had been carefully crafted to include an interesting mix of bidders and attendees from past auctions, including the private clients of distinguished galleries. This list was handed over to the pre-sales team, whose job it was to confirm background information provided on the different people, understand their level of interest in art and the artists whose works were to be showcased at the auction. By the end of the exercise, the sales team had pruned the list significantly. Face-to-face meetings were held with the top 100 people on this new, curated list, to educate them on the lineage and provenance of the different artworks and to assuage their interest in specific ones to be showcased at the auction. These discussions were carefully documented and passed on to the auctioneer, along with any queries received regarding the condition of specific works.

Benjamin Bell was the auctioneer tonight. Jay had met him a couple of times before. He was the best in the trade, having sold three out of the top ten paintings in the world over the past two decades. He knew how to create excitement and tempo. He operated much like a lap dancer, caressing and teasing his audience, keeping them on the edge of their seats while still ensuring decorum in the room.

'Only 10 per cent of those waiting in the hall are bidders,' said Benjamin, sipping his whisky.

'And the remaining 90 per cent?' asked his assistant, puzzled.

'Freeloaders,' said Benjamin, smiling. 'They need to be entertained.'

'Really, why?'

'Because if I don't have them jumping in excitement, cheering every bid, the active bidders will lose interest. Everyone likes an audience, especially those spending hundreds of thousands of dollars,' he smiled.

Benjamin knew his performance had to be excellent tonight; there was no margin for error. He had been rehearsing his speech for the past hour: 'Mr Gandhi on my left, sir, would you be kind enough to start the bid on this exemplary piece of art,' he said, taking a peek at his black diary.

This magical diary contained critical details not only on the lots being presented but also seating arrangements of important clients and their preferences. When a particular lot came up for sale, Benjamin would know who was interested in it beforehand and use this knowledge to make specific queries, often coaxing one collector to bid against another.

He was the master of the ring. He charmed the bidders and created the impression that the paintings were within their grasp. He teased them, knowing full well that only one of them would be the final victor. But instead of feeling dejected by their loss, under Benjamin's spell, the bidders felt even more committed to winning the next lot by bidding higher. The fiercer the fight and participation, the higher the bids and the greater the sense of victory for the winner. Benjamin could tell when a collector needed cajoling and time to make another bid. He could also identify those who were disciplined and could not be sweet-talked into bidding a penny more.

When Benjamin conducted an auction, one thing was certain: he would extract the last possible bid from the auction room before throwing down the hammer and announcing the victor.

As Jay glanced through the auction catalogue, he could see immediately that the sale was orchestrated to ensure maximum participation and guarantee the highest bids. There was no point in keeping important lots at the beginning of the auction when participants were still settling down, acclimatising themselves, women adjusting their blouses while men pulled on their trousers scratching their balls. It was the smaller lots with lower expected prices that were auctioned off right at the beginning, building momentum and tempo. These were followed by those artworks that were likely to meet or exceed their expected value, generating excitement and creating auction fever. The most sought after works of artists like V.S. Gaitonde, Tyeb Mehta, M.F. Husain and S. H. Raza were clubbed together in Lots 60 to 68, the painting by Rabindranath Tagore strategically placed between them at Lot 65. Artworks which were considered difficult to sell were placed right after well-known lots which were expected to evince interest and feverish bidding. This was the case with some works that were placed in Lots 69, 70 and 71. Similarly, in the case of two artworks by the same artist, the one enjoying greater prestige was kept first, the other introduced later. A well-known Mehta was slotted for Lot 10, followed by another, less-known one in Lot 11.

Even the seating arrangements were strategically planned. While most well-known art connoisseurs, critics, collectors and investors were seated in the front rows, a few were placed at the back to ensure even participation from all corners of the room. Collectors who were known to feverishly bid against each other were tactically placed together. Other high visibility areas such as the aisle seats in the middle of the auction room were occupied by dealers expected to bid actively. Under Benjamin's watchful eyes, the stage was set for a battle royale, a massacre that would create headlines the next day.

Jay was seated in his regular place, a few rows from the front, right by the aisle. He had used his influence to get a front row seat reserved for his client, Deepak Patel, a successful industrialist but a newbie in the art world. Seated among the art snobs in the front row, Deepak stood out like a sore thumb. The snobs represented the insiders of the art community and the auction was an opportunity for them to display their aristocracy, patronage and taste. They hugged and air-kissed, feverishly discussing both established and upcoming artists, dropping names generously. This insider group was a key influencer in the art community, the self-proclaimed guardians of high culture and taste. The exclusive club met regularly at auctions, openings of new art galleries or art exhibitions. They belonged to the same social group, lived in similar, posh neighbourhoods and had attended the same elite schools and colleges.

Jay looked at the well-dressed men and women and smiled to himself. They may have been the art doyens but there was another breed of investor coming up now—first-generation entrepreneurs who had amassed significant wealth in new age industries—who wanted a share of the art world. Deepak was one of them.

Jay recalled how a completely unknown person had stolen

the show at a Sotheby's auction a few years ago. Dressed casually in a blazer and sitting at the back of the room, this middle-aged man had broken all auction norms by bidding aggressively for Picasso's *Dora Maar au Chat*, a 1941 portrait that was the main attraction of the night. As he waived his paddle furiously in the air driving the price to $65 million (the estimate price being $50 million), his competitors started dropping away. No one knew the identity of this mysterious buyer who had bid a staggering $95.2 million for the painting by the time the hammer finally fell. Had Sotheby's known him, he would have certainly graced the front rows of the auction room.

One thing was clear, he was certainly new to auctions, otherwise he would not have participated in the bidding process so early on, nor would he have waved his paddle with such ferocity.

Jay usually avoided being present at auctions himself, choosing to operate discreetly via the phone. This was a practice adopted by dealers who preferred to keep the identity of their clients hidden. At a Sotheby auction a few years earlier, a very well-known dealer in the art circles was bidding via his mobile phone on behalf of his client for Picasso's *Garcon a la Pipe*. As the bidding intensified and reached in excess of $75 million, this dealer's face suddenly turned white, his nervousness obvious to all. Unknown to the auctioneer, his phone battery had died. A little bewildered, the auctioneer asked him if he needed more time. The dealer snatched his neighbour's phone and dialled his client frantically to re-enter the bidding process at $77 million. Eventually, the dealer's client was the under-bidder with the painting selling for a record $104 million, the highest for a Picasso work and a world record at the time. Jay wondered what would have happened had the dealer not remembered the phone number of his client, a highly plausible scenario in today's age of technology.

Jay was hoping a few records would be broken tonight as well. He had made a personal appearance because his client specifically wanted him to bid for a work by Rabindranath Tagore, one of the Navaratnas slotted for Lot 65.

Benjamin greeted the gathered crowd and began the auction. Smaller lots by Ram Kumar, Husain, Gaitonde and Raza were hammered away for between $50,000 and $200,000, creating excitement. It was almost as if the last boat was leaving town and everyone wanted to be on it. The ones making the maximum noise were regular bidders but seldom buyers. They wanted to be seen bidding by other participants but their intention was never to get caught at the end of the line. It was all a show of prestige.

Benjamin cleared his throat ever so subtly as he introduced Lot 10, a much sought-after masterpiece by Tyeb Mehta. He knew that there were six well-known collectors of Tyeb Mehta in the room; seven enquiries had been received regarding the condition report of the artwork and, most importantly, a Mr Diwan from Delhi had lost out the last time this artwork had been showcased at an auction almost a decade ago. Would Diwan let the painting slip from his hands again? Not if Benjamin could help it.

The bidding began at $600,000 and increased in lots of 100,000 till it reached $1.5 million. It slowed down considerably after that. Benjamin knew that there was still one last bid to be had from Mr Diwan. He coaxed him to bid just a little more to ensure that he didn't go back empty-handed. After all, who knew when this painting would come up for auction again? Would he lose out again for want of a few thousand dollars? Finally, the hammer fell at $1.55 million and Mr Diwan emerged the proud and happy owner of the Tyeb Mehta.

Gradually, the tempo increased along with the pitch of Benjamin's voice. People could feel the rising anxiety levels in the room. Some were sweating, others were at the edge of their seats, but there were still others like Jay who sat comfortably, not impacted by the environment. Deepak Patel did not display a similar cool, instead jumping in his seat out of excitement, much to the annoyance of his neighbours.

After a few popular contemporary paintings had been sold, the first of the Navaratnas was introduced at Lot 30, a painting by renowned nineteenth-century artist Raja Ravi Varma. This was followed by five others at Lots 34, 37, 38, 45 and 51. Jay was happy to see the reception that they received. It was apparent that the auction house had done a good pre-sales job. The museum he had introduced earlier had finally won three out of the four paintings it had bid for but at prices much higher than expected. If this was any indication, then the last painting by Tagore would be aggressively bid.

As the auction progressed, the atmosphere in the room became electric. At Lot 63, a much sought-after Gaitonde was introduced. Feverish bidding led to the hammer finally falling at $3.8 million, setting a new record for contemporary artwork in India. Even before the audience had a chance to settle back down, Benjamin introduced Lot 64, a large acrylic on canvas from Tyeb Mehta's Mahishasura collection. He gave a satisfied smile when he ultimately sold it for $3.2 million.

At last, Lot 65 arrived, the artwork of legendary writer, poet, philosopher and artist Rabindranath Tagore. The untitled painting was a portrait of a veiled woman with a melancholy expression. Jay knew that the exuberance created in the room by the sale of Gaitonde and Mehta was definitely going to rub off on the bidding for this lot.

He remained calm as the bidding began. He knew that Benjamin was aware of his interest in this painting and he kept looking in his direction. He waited for the initial excitement and tempo to calm down, then right when one of the other bidders thought that the painting was within his grasp, Jay signalled his interest with a slight movement of his hand. Most others would have raised their paddle, but not him. He was an insider, too well known in this circle. His gesture was immediately noticed by the spotter who stood at the side of the room.

'We have a new bid here, sir,' announced the spotter.

Benjamin couldn't hide his smile. Jay had finally entered his ring and as the ring master, he was going to make him pay for it. The front rows turned back to see who this new entrant was. Animated discussions and loud whispers could be heard from all corners of the room.

Jay entered the bidding at $300,000. He was almost immediately overbid at $350,000, which he countered again at $400,000, drawing much cheering and applause from the crowd.

Just as Jay was settling down in his seat, smug in the knowledge that the painting was his, there was a counter-offer of $450,000. The noise level in the room went up perceptibly. The art doyens surrounding Deepak Patel had their eyes glued on Jay. He knew there was only one question on everyone's lips, 'Will he? Won't he?'

But Jay was in no such dilemma. His instructions were clear: buy the Tagore regardless of price. And so with a slight gesture of his hand, Jay made the counter-bid at $475,000. Benjamin called out to the room for any counter-offers at $500,000 and waited for a few moments to allow people to gasp and collect themselves. He once again called for any counter-bids at $485,000, and then after a few moments, he slammed the auction hammer on the table, announcing the sale to Jay Malhotra at $475,000, a new record for the work of Rabindranath Tagore.

When the auction ended, Jay reached out to his client, congratulating him on his magnificent purchase. Deepak had wanted to be identified as the buyer of the work in front of the larger auction room. It didn't matter to him that the painting had been bought at nearly $150,000 over the estimated price. What mattered was that he had made a grand entrance, one that had been seen by the most exclusive art circles in the country. When the very same people who had ignored him at the beginning of the auction came over to congratulate him and ask his opinion of Tagore's work, Deepak knew he had arrived on the art scene.

By the end of the evening, all eighty pieces of art had been sold with three setting new records. Collectively, the patrons had shelled out nearly $16 million. There was no doubt that the auction had been a grand success.

Jay was relieved. The new benchmarks set by the Navaratnas would help cool the nerves of those clients who were heavily invested in their success and stability. But there was no time to rest. Every day presented a new challenge. There were too many sellers in the Navaratna market, but buyers were few and far between. He didn't see the broad smile on Patty's face as she left the auction room, otherwise he would have been worried.

Chapter 2

The Alpha Male

It was the summer of 1999 and the whole world waited anxiously for the Y2K bug to strike. No one knew what would happen when the clock struck twelve on the penultimate night. The largest corporations in the world had spent hundreds of billions of dollars in creating contingency plans, disaster recovery systems and whatever else the technology companies sold them.

Jay Malhotra, the youngest partner in the firm, sat beside his boss, Samir Aggarwal, as the limousine crawled through the morning traffic of Mumbai towards Nariman Point.

'Samir, I am convinced that all this paranoia about Y2K is a sham,' said Jay.

'What do you mean, it's a sham?' asked Samir.

'Well, it's nothing more than a marketing gimmick,' replied Jay. 'I can bet that these technology companies are behind this paranoia.'

'Now you are bullshitting.'

'So, let's have a bet then,' said Jay. 'If I lose, I will give you my watch and vice versa.'

'Why not?' replied Samir.

Jay smiled, 'Please keep your watch handy on New Year's, and I will personally come to collect it.'

'By the way, whom are we meeting today?' asked Samir.

'We are meeting Mr Oswal,' replied Jay. 'He is a textile king.'

'Is there anything you need to brief me on before the meeting?' asked Samir.

'Not required. It's all cool.'

'Then why am I accompanying you for this meeting?' asked Samir. 'I have other important things to attend to.'

'Well, this Oswal fellow is an old-timer. He insisted on meeting with the owner of the firm and that happens to be you. Don't worry, I will do all the talking at the meeting but your presence is required. I just need you to nod your head in concurrence with my recommendation.'

'I am certainly the owner of this firm and if you harbour ambitions of becoming a co-owner, then you will need to carry some people along with you, make some friends in the office. As of now, no one in the office likes you.'

'Samir, I am not here to win a popularity contest. I am here to make a successful career and earn a lot of money for both of us. Ambitious people like me who are fast risers seldom have friends. I have come to live with that. Friendship is a sacrifice I am willing to make if it helps me achieve my goals. After all, the bonus is dependent on my performance and not on the number of friends I have.'

The last statement had merit. In the financial world, the only thing that mattered was performance. Samir knew that despite his personal shortcomings, Jay was the best resource he had. He was aggressive and fiercely competitive, a go-getter who accounted for almost 40 per cent of the revenues for the firm, far more than what any other partner contributed. Samir didn't like the direction in which the discussion was going and decided to change the subject.

'How did you become so competitive and money-minded?' asked Samir.

'As the third child in a lower-middle-class family, I never had the luxury of choice. I didn't have any options to fall back on,' replied Jay. 'I knew from an early age that I had to chart my own future. Circumstances and survival instincts made me what I am.

'When I was in Class 10, I managed to get admission into a top-notch school at Mussoorie with a full scholarship. The school was very competitive; the best students from across India filled its classrooms. I still remember how in the morning assembly, the principal would repeat the same speech, week after week. "There are no accolades for coming second in life. Being good is not good enough, the problem with being good is that it isn't great."

'And then his last line would be like a hammer, "Does anyone remember the name of the second man to land on the moon?"

'Samir, had I been a part of the Apollo Mission to put a man on the moon, let me assure you, no one would have ever known Neil Armstrong. As regards to being money-minded, I understand the importance and value of money. Perhaps, more than anyone else. My father was an upright, honest manager in a nationalised bank. As a result, we seldom had money in the house. However, while he didn't earn money, he did earn a lot of goodwill and made a lot of friends. Friends he hoped would come in handy in his hour of need.

'However, post his retirement, when my mother was diagnosed with cancer, no such help ever came. He realised to his disappointment that all his friendships and goodwill had ended the day he retired. We were left to fend for ourselves and had to sell ancestral property to make good the financial costs associated with the medical treatment of my mother. That was the day I realised the importance of money. Unfortunately, it was too late for my mother, who could not be saved. I often wonder what would have happened had we organised the finances earlier. I then knew that money is your only friend in bad times and a bank balance is more tangible than goodwill.'

'I apologise, Jay. It wasn't my intention to make you relive that difficult phase of your life,' said Samir.

'No need to apologise,' replied Jay. 'It is important to be reminded of those times; it ensures that I remain focused.'

There was silence in the car as Jay looked outside the window in a pensive mood.

Samir's thoughts meanwhile drifted to the day he had interviewed Jay in college. Even then the boy had a fire in his belly and aggression in his eyes.

'Where do you see yourself in ten years, son?' he had asked.

'Occupying your chair, sir,' Jay had replied.

He had always been a fast learner. He quickly learnt the

basic rules of engagement in the financial world, where mistakes were not forgiven and careers ended even before they started:

1. Never pick up a ringing phone. You don't know who is on the other end.

2. Never give a client verbal advice. It is open to misinterpretation and, more importantly, if it hasn't been recorded it can't be billed.

3. Always cover your ass—it doesn't matter whether you are standing, sitting or bending down.

On his first assignment, a merger integration, there was hardly any expectations from him since he was the junior-most member of the team. His seniors often bullied him by making him get their coffee, find documents and photocopy back-up files. But Jay was not deterred. He remained focused, constantly pestering them with questions and reading up on the industry's best practices.

Late one evening, after his colleagues had left for the day, Jay was smoking outside the office when he ran into the CFO, the chief financial officer, of the company. The poor guy looked harrowed. He seemed to have run out of cigarettes and Jay was quick to come to his rescue, offering him a light. They spoke briefly that night. Jay must have made quite an impression on him because after that, the CFO came looking for him every time he wanted to go out for a smoke.

A few weeks after the assignment had ended, Samir had called Jay to his office to congratulate him. He remembered telling him, 'You created quite an impression on him, lad. It's not often that the CFO of such a large organisation remembers a junior analyst by name.'

'Thank you, sir,' Jay had replied.

'But there is one problem. You look your age.'

'I don't understand, sir.'

'The CFO was surprised that someone so young was part of a team handling business worth millions of dollars.'

The next day, he had asked the accounts department to release an advance of six months' salary to Jay with the following note: 'Buy a pair of branded spectacles. They will add a few years to your age and experience. Get a Zegna suit to look smart and well-kept and a limited edition Mont Blanc pen to look successful. If you look successful, no one will ever ask you what your age is again.'

His thoughts were broken midway by the voice in his head.

'Samir, please wake up,' said Jay. 'We have reached Maker Chambers. The entire top brass is waiting for us upstairs.'

They went directly to the boardroom, Jay leading the way. After exchanging pleasantries and visiting cards, they got straight down to business.

'What is the problem, Mr Oswal?' asked Jay.

'We need money.'

'Don't we all,' he replied with a smile. 'But, let us first analyse our current financial position before we try to find a solution.

'Your balance sheet is weak, you are highly leveraged and both your sales and gross margins are consistently declining. No bank in their right mind would ever lend a penny to you. And for the same reasons, no institution would ever invest equity in your company either.'

Jay paused for few seconds, allowing everyone inside the room to absorb his words. He could sense the environment in the room changing gradually, the mood becoming very poignant, as if everyone was attending a funeral procession. It was important to drub the client before showing him the light at the end of the tunnel. Only then did they truly value your advice and agree to your fees without negotiating on the amount.

After about half a minute, Mr Oswal asked, 'But is there a solution?'

'Of course there is, sir,' replied Jay smiling. 'But not an easy one. You will have to do as I tell you. We are in an era of technology and dotcom. No one gives a shit about a boring textile business. You will have to re-invent yourself. Hire a few software engineers and start a new department.'

'But we know nothing about software,' said Mr Oswal. 'How can we start a new business? This is suicidal.'

Jay shook his head in disagreement.

'It doesn't matter that you don't know anything about software, all I ask is that you hire a few software engineers and start a new department. I don't care if the business does not generate revenue. Give me a new story, something I can sell and then leave it to me. I will get your money. One more thing, please add the word "technology" in the name of your company.'

The room came alive; people were now sporting broad smiles where only a minute ago there had been only grim faces. They had finally understood what was required of them. They didn't have to actually develop a new business. They only needed to do enough so as to create the perception that they did.

Chapter 3

The Art Forger

It was the middle of the night in the year 1966 in a small house in the suburbs of Mumbai. The entrance to the attic was locked from inside. If you put your ear against the door, you could hear the faint murmurs of a drunk man rumbling verses in Bengali, a language which only a few months earlier was alien to him.

The attic was dark and dingy; a single bulb flickered in a corner, fighting a losing battle against the pervading darkness. There was dirt everywhere, cobwebs hung from the ceiling. At one end lay a single cot which had seen better days. Next to it was a half-empty plate with food a few days old. Empty bottles lay littered around the room along with a few half-eaten fruits. The air was stale. There was an all-pervasive smell, difficult to describe, a concoction of alcohol, sweat and rotten food.

At the other end of the attic lay many paintings. Portraits of heavily veiled women surrounded by darkness, sad faces;

grey and dark backgrounds reflecting the sorrow and darkness in his subconscious mind. The portraits had one common feature, the intense and piercing gaze that burned the viewer's soul and unravelled his deepest secrets. Then there were the landscapes with flowing rivers, vegetation and greenery, expressing freedom without boundaries and the free flow of ideas in his mind.

A few feet away from the paintings lay several piles of paper. Ordinary paper, the kind on which you saw a child draw, except that this paper was a few decades old, and had been specifically sourced from old printing presses and galleries. Next to it lay a pile of paintings of street artists belonging to the early twentieth century. These were no masterpieces, they had not been sourced for their artistic craftsmanship but for their frames. These frames had been carefully opened and their dust preserved, ready to receive their new masterpieces.

It was a challenge to decipher the words that came out of his mouth, as he half sang and mumbled. However, if you knew Bengali maybe you could. They were from the 'First Sorrow', a poem written by Nobel Laureate Rabindranath Tagore in remembrance of his sister-in-law Kadambari Devi, who committed suicide a few months after his marriage. Tagore described her suicide as his 'first permanent acquaintance with death.' He wrote:

'With the loosening of the attraction of the world, the beauty of nature took on for me a deeper meaning.'

While physically he appeared intoxicated, his mind was alert as he stood in front of the empty canvas, a brush in hand, waiting anxiously for the moment to arrive. And then it did—he found himself standing in the serene environs of Shantiniketan, his hands moving desperately, trying to capture the last rays of the falling sun, much like his master many decades earlier. However, despite his best efforts neither the size of the canvas nor the speed of his brush could capture the waves of continuously evolving thoughts in his mind, keeping him uneasy.

He stood there wearing a white kurta-pyjama, sporting long hair and a longer beard. The sleeves of his kurta were smeared with vegetative colours of brown and black, used as a brush to capture the moment when there was none in his hand. There were dark circles under his eyes; insomnia was his friend and constant companion. He looked frail and weak due to inadequate consumption of food and water and excessive alcohol.

You would not be wrong in describing Arun as a 'Master Forger'. He possessed exceptional raw artistic talent, an understanding of art history and experience in frame-making and restoration. However, he did not see himself as a forger. He was an artist and his creations were masterpieces.

He did not make cheap imitations. Those were below his dignity, disrespectful and demeaning to his talent. Instead, he used his knowledge, talent and imagination to interpret the works of Tagore by filling gaps in his body of work. He either created new artworks which reflected the mood and theme of works done by the Grand Master at specific phases in his life or he recreated artworks that were mentioned in various archives but were lost or destroyed by the passage of time. These artworks seldom had descriptions, being known often by just their name. Where descriptions were available, Arun created his masterpieces based on his interpretation of the descriptions; in other cases, he let his imagination take over, seeking influence from other works of the Grand Master available from the same period.

He had spent a greater part of the previous year studying everything there was to learn about the Master. His travels had taken him across the length and breadth of Bengal. He visited places of historical importance which had influenced the emergence of the Bengal School, an influential art movement that originated primarily in Kolkata and flourished throughout India during the early twentieth century.

He spent weeks in the archives of the Government College of Arts and Craft, the pioneering institution which spearheaded the Bengal School, going through old records, books and documentation on the lives of important artists from this period to understand how they evolved, the key influences in their lives and how this evolution impacted their individual styles of painting.

Why did he choose Tagore over others? Was it his larger-than-life personality? Or did he find solace in the darkness that was omnipresent in Tagore's paintings, death being a constant companion in his life?

Whatever the reason, Arun travelled to Shantiniketan, the abode of learning created by Tagore and enrolled himself at Kala Bhavan, the school of fine arts. Rabindra Bhavan and Kala Bhavan between themselves held almost 60 per cent of Tagore's known oeuvre of 2,500 paintings. They were the most important source of information on understanding the individual style of the artist, his brush movement, formation of lines and usage of colours. They gave him an insight into the different subjects that formed the core of the Grand Master's work and how they had evolved over time. He also understood the different mediums that were used by the Grand Master in pursuit of his creations.

He spent as much time as possible interacting with the local people of Shantiniketan, particularly those who had lived with Tagore or knew of him. He wanted to absorb the culture of the city, understand its people, their daily lives, difficulties, likes, dislikes and ambition.

He wanted to relive the life of the Grand Master, feel his anxieties, difficulties, excitement and encouragement. He tried to emulate the daily schedule of the Grand Master, getting up early in the morning to capture the first rays of the sun on his canvas, attending the school, interacting with students and peers and returning to the comfort of his hostel only to return just before sunset to once again catch the last rays of the dying sun on his canvas. Shantiniketan had remained in a time warp; not much had changed in its spirit and culture. You could still get a glimpse into life and travails as they existed in the first half of the twentieth century. He carefully catalogued all the information, making descriptive notes about his feelings and expressions.

He had just finished another landscape using pencils, both lead and colour, water colours, ink and some pigments extracted from leaves and vegetables. He had made the painting in a single sitting, using a combination of pen, brush and on several occasions, his fingertips. And like his Master, he was impatient. He never used oils, they took just too damn long to dry. Oh, and there were seldom any greens and reds in the landscapes. The Grand Master, you see, was colour blind, using dark chocolate and black profusely. However, this did not imply that there wasn't any zing and colour in his paintings. He loved the use of sharp highlight crayons, experimental corrosive inks, golden yellow being his favourite colour.

The brush style had cross knots and wild brush movements with more emphasis on expression and usage of colour than line formations and specific descriptions of form. Like his master, Arun's hands could seldom keep pace with the evolving thoughts and expressions in his mind, resulting in wild brush movements.

In order to truly appreciate and recreate the works of his Grand Master, he had read all his poems and writings. Only then could one comprehend the context and background of the paintings, appreciate the depth of the characters and understand the complete picture. The Grand Master used his writings and paintings to express his deep, unexplained feelings and emotions. He was an expressionist, who was fascinated by the different forms in the world and used colours as a bridge between the world of forms and the world of ideas. Since he had not received any formal education in the discipline of art, his style of painting was unique and free-flowing, not restrained by any training or tradition but by the thoughts in his mind which were rhythmic, with harmonious combination of lines and colours.

Hidden in the confines of the attic in a state of intoxication, Arun enjoyed the opportunity to live his dreams of becoming an artist and impersonating the character of his Grand Master. However, no sooner did the effect of the alcohol wane, that his smile disappeared, faced with the harsh realities of life where he was a failed artist and nothing more. This constant conflict between reality and his imaginary world pulled him in opposite directions, making him restless and uneasy. Alcohol, which he had resorted to as a means to relive Tagore's life, gradually became a deeper companion as it helped him overcome his loneliness, his failure as an artist, the loss of his father and to some extent, his own guilt.

≈

Chapter 4

Holy Shit!

J ay switched off the alarm. It was five in the morning, time for him to start his daily schedule. It didn't matter to him that it was the first day of January and that the entire world slept, affected by the overindulgence of the previous evening. He planned to call his boss at eight and remind him about their morning meeting. He had won the bet, the Y2K bug had turned out to be a big sham, as he had predicted. It was time for him to collect his winnings. He didn't intend on taking Samir's watch but wanted to remind him of his loss, the watch on his hands a constant reminder as to who was in control.

As he lazily stretched in bed, his arms felt the warmth of the woman sleeping next to him. He confirmed her name; she was called Tina. He had met her at a bar in Bandra the previous evening. He didn't know who she was, possibly because he had forgotten but more likely because he had never asked. He knew her name only because he had scribbled it on his left palm, a habit that he had inculcated with experience. Tina was beautiful, the kind of woman who turned heads in a bar. She was attracted to him, maybe because he was well groomed with short hair, manicured nails and a shining face; or perhaps because he was physically fit, capable of finishing a marathon in under three hours with a washboard stomach; or maybe because she saw him drive up to the bar in a Maserati. Whatever the reason, he was extremely popular amongst women. However, in his fast-paced, work-centred life, he had no time or inclination to entertain commitments. Consequently, women walked in and out of his life at regular intervals, as would Tina later that day.

Last night he came home at two in the morning. This was an aberration in his otherwise disciplined life, where he was fast asleep by ten in the night. After coming back from the office, he would do a quick workout with his personal trainer followed by an early dinner consisting of proteins and greens. By half past eight, he would be in his den listening to blues music, reading books and unwinding. The only time he made an exception was when he was either entertaining a client or chasing a woman he found intriguing.

He got out of bed and wrote a note to Tina: 'Tina, thanks for making the night memorable... J.P.S. My man Friday, Rajesh, will attend to anything you require.'

Experience had taught him to leave a personal note. It helped the women overcome their day-after guilt and feel reassured about their self-esteem when they woke up in the morning.

He quickly brushed his teeth, flossed and gargled before

changing into his running gear and going for a 10-kilometre jog. He loved running at Marine Drive in the morning, from Chowpatty to the Oberoi and back. The morning breeze made him relax, opened his mind and helped him plan his day.

The last six months had been extremely good. He was featured on the cover page of a leading business magazine as one of the fastest rising stars in the banking circles in India. The article talked about his unorthodox deals and style of functioning. While the article gave him the necessary publicity, highlighting his achievements, it also identified him as a potential target in the eyes of the regulators. So far, Jay had successfully eluded the regulator by staying ahead of the curve. His deals had made tons of money for the firm and his clients who sweared allegiance to him. However, every round of success further fuelled his risk-taking appetite. He had become complacent and a sense of invincibility had set in.

As advised by him, Mr Oswal had made the necessary cosmetic changes to transition his textile business into a technology powerhouse by hiring a few software engineers and changing the name of his organisation. He had also acquired his own shares through unaffiliated investment firms, increasing his unofficial stake in his company while simultaneously reducing the supply of shares in the market.

Jay, on his part, had successfully marketed the transition story to his high-networth clients, stimulating demand for the shares of the company. The shares of the company had been on a roll, rising by over 200 per cent in the last few months. Institutional investors who had so far kept to the sidelines, could no longer ignore the party and had jumped in, less out of their conviction in the transition story and more out of their greed and fear of missing out on the rally, thereby providing Jay's high-networth clients a profitable exit.

Everything was going according to his plan. It was only a matter of time before retail investors took the bait, seduced by the exponential rise in the price of the shares. Their greed would provide both the institutional investors and Mr Oswal with an exit route.

This was a foolproof mechanism which had worked on numerous occasions in the past. Thanks to this plan, Jay would successfully raise money for Mr Oswal outside the balance sheet of the company. Mr Oswal could then use this money as he deemed fit.

As he got back home, a glass of lemon water mixed with salt and sugar awaited his arrival. He gulped it down and rushed into the shower. He hoped to see Tina awake. Maybe she could join him to make an otherwise mundane shower experience more pleasurable. However, it wasn't his lucky day as she was still fast asleep. A little disappointed, he showered alone and then went into the changing room. His wardrobe reflected his organised, disciplined life. A dozen white and light blue shirts hung neatly in a row, the corresponding undergarments kept by their side. Five different suits hung on the other side: pinstripes, black, dark blue, charcoal and grey, matching shoes below them with the matching socks inside. He had an interesting collection of ties. Those that dangled at one end of the road were rather sober, meant for client meetings and on the other end hung crimson red ties which he loved wearing to the office. They reflected his aggressive and fiercely competitive nature. His cufflinks and watches were neatly arranged in a jewellery box kept in the corner.

Today he wanted something more casual and pulled out a pair of jeans along with a collared T-shirt from the top shelf. His keen eyesight immediately picked up changes in the set-up; someone had messed with his clothes. He was finicky about these things and was very annoyed.

He went back into the living room to read the morning newspapers; he read three of them as part of his morning schedule. Rajesh had already prepared his breakfast, which lay on the dining table. He had eaten the same breakfast his entire working life. It consisted of a double egg white omelette and a slice of multigrain bread along with a glass of skimmed milk.

As he finished breakfast, he called Rajesh. 'Tell the maid not to touch my wardrobe again,' he said. 'This is the second time it has happened. I will fire her if it happens again.'

Rajesh knew what this meant; the maid was on her way out like many before her. However, since he paid them more than anyone else in the building, there was no shortage of them.

'And one more thing, Tina madam is sleeping inside,' he added. 'Make sure she is not disturbed. In case she requires something, help her out.'

Rajesh nodded his head. He knew what needed to be done. He would make a large glass of orange juice. They generally liked that after a booze-filled long night. If that didn't help, then a double espresso shot would do. After they were wide awake, he would prepare breakfast for them, generally eggs with sausages and bacon, and finally, he would call a cab.

More often than not, he never saw them again.

Jay looked at his watch. It was eight. Time to call Samir.

'Happy New Year, Samir!' he said.

'What time is it?'

'It's eight, time for you to wake up.'

'Couldn't you wait?'

'I did, for three long hours. Please get ready. I am coming over in an hour, and by the way, that Y2K shit was a sham. An exceptionally well-executed marketing sham, mind you, maybe we can learn something from it?'

An hour later, Jay was ringing the bell at Samir's house. Samir was dressed in a casual T-shirt and tracks, his hair all over the place, obviously not fully awake. They sat down in the living room and exchanged pleasantries.

'I could use some espresso,' said Samir, still rubbing his eyes. 'Would you like some coffee?'

'No thanks,' replied Jay.

As Samir walked back with a cup of steaming espresso in his hand, he said, 'Oh! I almost forgot, please take this.' He pulled out a carefully packed box from under the table. 'This contains the watch.'

Jay looked at him in amazement.

'Obviously, you didn't pack this in the morning,' said Jay.

'Obviously not,' replied Samir. 'This box has been lying packed for the past six months.'

'So you knew that I was going to win all this time.'

Samir smiled. Suddenly, winning didn't seem that sweet anymore.

'I didn't intend on taking the watch prior to coming to

your house but now I gladly will,' replied Jay, a little annoyed. 'Anyway, now that you are awake, let's get down to discussing business.'

'So, when do I get that promotion I have been eyeing for the past two years?' he asked.

'You will, in some time,' replied Samir. 'You are still too young. The other partners will be up in arms.'

'But I will always be younger than them. This is not fair. You didn't consider my age when you were deciding on the annual targets.'

He could hear his phone continuously ringing in the background, but he didn't wish to interrupt his current discussion. He had Samir pinned against the wall and was enjoying every moment.

'I have delivered higher numbers than any other partner for three years in a row now. I deserve that promotion.'

'Jay, do you want to take that call?' asked Samir.

'No, it must be someone calling me to wish me Happy New Year. It's only half past ten in the morning,' he replied.

'But it could be someone from the market. You do remember that they are open today, don't you?'

He glanced at his phone, it was one of his fund managers.

'Happy New Year, mate!' he said.

'Are you kidding? You fucking bastard.'

'Hey! Easy, man. What happened?'

'You don't know? You son of a bitch. That technology stock you made us buy a fortnight ago is down by twenty per cent, on a lower circuit, with a huge sell order. I look like an idiot in front of my investment committee. Make no mistake,

Jay Malhotra, if I go down, I will burn you.'

The line was disconnected.

'I need to leave, Samir.'

Samir could sense that something was a miss.

'What happened?' he asked.

'I don't know yet. But I need to leave now.'

As soon as he stepped out, he called up his office to get the latest position on the stock. It was down by 20 per cent, on a lower circuit, with no buyers and an outstanding sell order of over a million shares.

Who could be selling he wondered. It couldn't be the institutions. The poor bastards had entered the stock only a fortnight back. He needed answers quickly before it turned into a nightmare and only one person could provide them. He dialled Mr Oswal's number.

'Who the fuck is selling the stock?' he asked.

Mr Oswal was taken aback by the use of the foul language, but Jay didn't care.

'I don't know,' replied Oswal.

'Don't bullshit, Mr Oswal,' he said. 'It is someone in your camp. Find out who. Otherwise we will all be fucked.'

As soon as he disconnected the line, he got a call from another fund manager.

'What the fuck is happening, Jay?'

'Give me some time to find out. I am on it as we speak.'

'You better hurry, man, we are on very shaky ground here.'

He disconnected the line to take Mr Oswal's call.

'Who is it?' he asked.

'It's my estranged brother,' came the reply.

'You have a fucking estranged brother and you didn't think it fit to tell me. How many times did I ask you if all the shares were in your control? Anyway, how many shares does he have?' he asked.

'Ten per cent,' replied Oswal.

'Holy shit. You will have to buy these shares, Mr Oswal. There is no other way.'

'But I don't have the money, Mr Malhotra. You were supposed to organise it,' Oswal replied.

'Okay, let me see what I can do.'

As soon as he disconnected the call, he knew it was all over. He immediately analysed the list of funds which had invested based on his recommendation. There were two of them he liked. He called them both.

'I will make it up to you somewhere else,' he said. 'Get out of this stock if you can.'

For the next two weeks, the stock remained in a continuous downward circuit with only sellers and no buyers. The extreme volatility immediately caught the attention of the market regulator, who initiated an enquiry. There was intense heat with everyone running for cover.

By the time this episode subsided, there was substantial collateral damage. A few fund managers had lost their jobs, forced to resign by their investment committees. Further, for the first time, the regulator had managed to obtain a complaint against Jay from one of the clients who had lost heavily in this rout. However, despite their best efforts they still couldn't find evidence linking the firm to the fiasco. They wanted their pound of flesh and continued to hound the firm and its partners. They had to demonstrate that regulation was effective and the guilty paid for their misadventures, otherwise they risked losing the faith of the public at large. Eventually, they made an offer to Samir. It wasn't really an offer inasmuch as not giving him a choice. He was told to either give up his firm or sacrifice his shining star. He did what any successful businessman would have done.

≈

Chapter 5

Struggle! Hunger! I am an Artist

A run stood out in a crowd but not for the pleasant reasons that many people did. He was tall, thin and skinny. He was neither too fair nor too dark. He blended in with the crowd. It was easy not to notice him. But his passion for art made him lose his appetite and skimp on his sleep. He would forget to bathe and shave for weeks. It was because of his unkemptness that he stood out. People thought he was a homeless person on the streets of Mumbai and did their best to ignore him.

Arun belonged to a lower-middle-class Bengali family. Art and music were in his DNA. His grandfather had been a popular street painter in Kolkata in the early twentieth century and his grandmother was a known musician from the Benaras Gharana. While art and culture were respected and patronised by the rich and famous, the artists themselves lived very simple lives, wrapped up in their thoughts and creations with no time or inclination to pursue worldly matters. Their fame and glory was seldom reflected in financial well-being. Extreme poverty and financial pressure had forced his father to abandon his career midway as an artist. Instead, he had taken a desk job at the Kolkata College of Arts and Crafts, which offered him a meagre but steady monthly income. He had a burning desire to see his son succeed as an artist but knew from personal experience that a good artist wasn't always a successful one. His son had raw artistic talent, but would he be able to find buyers for his work?

As a child, Arun suffered from polio, which left a lingering effect on his right leg. While other children played in the Maidan or ran across the lawns of Victoria Memorial, Arun had stayed at home painting. On his tenth birthday, his father gave him a canvas and a box of oil paints. Two days later, he walked into Arun's room to see a painting showing children playing football on the Maidan. Arun had expressed his desire through the brush.

His immobility made him insecure and he felt inferior. The fact that other children teased him did not help matters. He was a lonely child, preferring the company of paints and canvasses to the garrulous company of other young boys.

In the early 1950s, Arun's family migrated to Mumbai. In the post-Independence era, Mumbai had overtaken Kolkata as the new centre for the development of art under the influence of the Progressive Artists' Group spearheaded by Husain, Raza and Souza. In Mumbai, Arun's father got a job at the Jehangir Art Gallery.

As a teenager in Mumbai, he fully exploited his father's administrative position at the Jehangir Art Gallery. He attended every function, exhibition and talk, even if it meant bunking school. He took odd jobs and volunteered during events to get unhindered access to artists and their work. He was full of energy after these events, excitedly discussing his observations with his father.

Despite his meagre income, Arun's father always provided for Arun's artistic passion, sometimes at the cost of annoying his wife. It wasn't that Arun's mother did not believe in his artistic talent but having seen her husband fail as an artist, she did not want to see her son lead a life of penury as well. But Arun's father had the faith that Arun would succeed where he had failed. He often told his wife that she didn't need to worry about savings; once Arun became a famous artist all their money troubles would be taken care of. While Arun appreciated the vote of confidence, he also felt the pressure of his father's blind faith.

After passing school, Arun joined the JJ School of Art at his father's encouragement. His father took a personal loan from friends and acquaintances to pay his fees. He hoped that the school would help bring structure and form to his son's raw talent. It was important for his son to study the great artists of the past and be inspired by their styles and techniques. The teaching at the JJ School of Art would help Arun hone his skills and add the panache required to take his art to the next level.

After graduating from the JJ School of Art, Arun spent the next five years trying his hand at becoming a successful artist. As no gallery was willing to show his work, he sold his paintings on the streets of Fort and Kala Ghoda. Some work was lapped up by friends and acquaintances, giving him a high. However, he soon accepted the constant struggle that defined the life of an artist. Money was always short. He was barely managing to make ends meet.

The art world is harsh and cruel. For every artist who becomes successful and gains recognition, there are several who die in poverty. Being talented is not good enough. Success requires business sense, marketing, networking and an element of luck. A successful artist need not necessarily possess extraordinary artistic talent; and exceptional artistic talent is not always a guarantee of achieving success. Arun saw many of his peers sacrificing originality and style to earn a living. They copied the works of the old masters. This meant doing the same paintings over and over again for the rest of their lives in styles that were alien to them. While it offended their artistic sensibilities, it was a necessary evil done to meet their daily expenses.

The demand for works of the old masters at pocket-friendly rates was so great that even hawkers who sold framed posters and prints made more money than artists like Arun, who stood by their originality and style. Arun didn't have it in him to market himself and his original work had no market. Had it not been for his father's constant encouragement, he would have stopped walking on this path years ago.

And so when, a few years later, his father unexpectedly passed away after a heart attack, he watched his life disintegrate before his eyes. He couldn't envision a life without his constant support and encouragement. He was lonely, his greatest influence and critic no longer by his side. His family didn't have any financial savings and within a fortnight of his father's death, Arun was forced to give up painting and take up odd jobs to provide for them. To add to his distress, friends from whom his father had borrowed money started hounding the family to get their money back.

Out of sympathy, one of his family friends managed to get him a job at a framing and art restoration shop. The job was a necessity to meet expenses; however, his mind remained restless, never at ease, the guilt of not being able to fulfil his father's dreams a constant presence. His mind wavered and he continued to indulge in artistic creations every night.

Within two years he had learnt the intricacies of art restoration, the structure of oil paintings and the interplay between various components such as the stretcher, canvas, primer, oil paint and varnish. This experience came handy as he restored a painting by Rabindranath Tagore which was in poor shape. Its varnish had become yellow, the paint had cracked and peeled off, revealing patches of the naked canvas. He applied a solvent to remove the varnish and in the process, softened the paint layer. He applied heat with an iron and 'facing' (small bits of paper pasted to identify areas which need restoration) all over the piece. Thereafter, he removed the canvas from the stretcher and applied a mixture of wax and resin to the back of the painting. As the wax and resin mix penetrated the canvas and came to the surface of the paint layer, it bound the entire structure together.

In addition to oil paints, Arun learnt how to restore old frames and deal with the restoration of watercolours on paper. The job kept him busy and financially stable.

One day, he was asked by a friend who worked with an architect to do an imitation of a popular painting by Raja Ravi Varma, one which depicted a mythological scene from the Mahabharata in which Draupadi was seen carrying a bowl of milk and honey. A few years earlier, he would have refused such an assignment. However, the passage of time had made him a wiser man. He accepted the assignment as a personal challenge and spent the next fortnight reading about the style and works of Raja Ravi Varma. He visited the Jehangir Art Gallery frequently to analyse a few of his works on display. He bought an old canvas from the bylanes of the Fort area and a frame which looked similar to some of those he had seen earlier at the gallery. Over the next few nights, he worked meticulously on copying Raja Ravi Varma's style and created an exact replica of the painting but for one key difference. He left his mark on the imitation by painting Draupadi in a sari which had a Bengali border.

His friend was extremely happy and paid him an amount equivalent to his monthly earnings at the shop. Arun soon realised he had a knack for creating imitations of popular works of the old masters and was much in demand by the architects in the city. However, he always left some impression of his work on the imitations to ensure that they were easily identifiable to an expert eye. These imitations gave him a steady flow of income in addition to his wages from the restoration shop. The money was more than sufficient to meet his needs and that of his family.

One day, while having a casual discussion with a friend from the art fraternity, Arun heard about Han Van Meegeren, a failed artist who had successfully created several forgeries of the great Dutch artist Johannes Vermeer.

Such was the quality of his artistry that even after he decided to confess and declare his forgeries, none in the art fraternity believed him. How could they? These were the same experts who had fallen over each other to announce these paintings as amongst the greatest finds of the twentieth century. Changing their expert opinion would have meant a loss of face and reputation for them. So they dug in their heels and stuck by their professional opinions given earlier on the matter and claimed that Meegeren was a liar, a traitor who had partnered with the Nazis in loot and plunder and was creating this plot around forgeries only to save his skin.

Faced with the death penalty, Meegeren requested the court to give him an opportunity to absolve himself of this charge by allowing him to create another of Vermeer's masterpieces. Surrounded by court-appointed experts and witnesses, he laboured over the next six weeks and finally succeeded in proving his innocence. He escaped the death penalty but was found guilty of fraud and sentenced to one year of imprisonment.

Arun noticed some stark similarities between himself and Meegeren. Like Meegeren, the art fraternity had discouraged him from pursuing his own work but every time he created an imitation of a known masterpiece, his work was appreciated and recognised. Were people evaluating the quality of the work or merely the signature of the artist at the bottom of the canvas? He felt anger and frustration at his failure to establish a name for himself. Influenced by Meegeren, he decided to hit back at the art critics and connoisseurs. Arun decided to quit the restoration shop and go back to Bengal where the Bengal School, an influential art movement, had emerged.

Chapter 6

The Cigar Connoisseur

Many people had gathered to attend a seminar on Tagore's paintings being conducted at the National Gallery of Modern Art, New Delhi. Biswas Mukherjee, a leading expert on the Bengal School and in particular on the oeuvre of Rabindranath Tagore, was officiating.

Patty, the owner of two successful art galleries, sat in the first row overlooking the dais. She was in attendance today because she was on the lookout for a suitable person to become the curator of her gallery. This position had fallen vacant a few months earlier when the last curator was unceremoniously fired, a victim of her ever expanding ego.

She had been closely following Biswas' research and was well versed with the views expressed in his articles, journals and public appearances. He was an alumnus of the JJ School of Art and had over 100 research articles to his credit. He had gained much of his repute while working as a research scholar at Shantiniketan.

While she had little doubt about Biswas' research credentials, what she really wanted to evaluate was his persona and stage presence. She had heard that he possessed a fine collection of cigars and single malts. Surely, a person with such fine tastes would have a persona. She didn't want a dumbass scholar who only rambled about art history but couldn't sell a single painting. She knew that art scholars and academics suffered from various idiosyncrasies. She wanted to find out whether these would be a hindrance in the performance of their commercial duties.

For example, Biswas was known to be a strong believer in the charm of the old way of dealing and despised the transformation of the art world into an industry and the corresponding commercialisation which had commoditised art aesthetics and connoisseurship, turning art into a measly investment asset. According to him, all that was old and good had been lost and all that remained was money. She didn't agree with his opinion. If there was no money then who would fund the research? she wondered. They had to go hand in hand. However, so long as his beliefs did not interfere with the daily working of the gallery, she didn't care.

Further, like most scholars, Biswas was passionate and overzealous about his accomplishments in the fields of art history and research. Any attempt to question his authority or beliefs was met with immediate reprisal. She knew that this was something she had to keep in mind, especially after losing her last curator.

She was pleasantly surprised when she saw him slowly walk up the dais to commence the lecture. He was dressed in a Bengali silk kurta-pyjama which was simple yet elegant in its appearance. If his speech was as good as his clothes, she would have found her curator.

As he commenced his lecture on the evolution of Rabindranath Tagore as a painter, she was overwhelmed by his accent. He spoke in a crisp Oxford accent and his language could put even the most exceptional writers to shame.

'The development of Tagore as a painter was closely associated with the correction of his manuscripts. While writing his poems, he would often make corrections by covering some words with ink and adding others. He would link these covered areas to create patterns, forms and designs. Thus he developed an interest in doodling and sketching.'

She raised her hand to ask a question but was declined.

'We will take questions at the end of this session,' responded Biswas politely. 'While these doodles and sketches were unplanned and shaped more by corrections and accidents, they seemed to be influenced by recollections of art objects that Tagore might have seen in books and museums during his extensive travels. It was only in 1928 that he started making independent paintings of animals. However, these animals appeared to be influenced more by mythology than the real world.

'His earlier works were based more on imagination and creativity than any sense of planned execution. He would project an animal on to an imagined body, or a human head on to an animal body and vice versa. However, all these forms were structured by the innate sense rhythm.'

He took a momentary pause to allow the audience an

opportunity to absorb and recollect their thoughts. After drinking some water, he began again...

'Tagore saw paintings as a vast procession of forms. It made him more observant and sensitive to nature and the outside world. This rendezvous with nature found expression in his landscapes. He would try and capture the natural surroundings under both the emerging and fading light of the sun, with joyful skies and forms setting into gloomy outlines that invoked mystery and ominous calm.

'Tagore never named his paintings. He didn't want to impose his literary imagination on the sensibilities of the viewers. He wanted the viewers to evaluate his paintings based on their own experiences and feelings.

'The human face was a constant feature in Tagore's work. As a theme, it appeared throughout his artistic career, demonstrating his unequivocal interest in human personae. As a writer, he was used to linking human appearance with the inner soul. Painting provided him a similar opportunity whereby he could turn the human face into a symbolic mask. Later, as his expressive skills grew, faces became more individualised. Shadows of faces he encountered or remembered began to find reflection in his paintings, giving them the echo and expansiveness of characters.'

As he finished the lecture, Biswas put down his reading glasses and looked up to face the audience. He announced that the forum was now open for questions. Patty was the first one to raise her hand. She had been anxiously waiting for this moment. She knew that she had to make the right first impression on him otherwise she wouldn't have a chance of winning him over. Unknown to anyone else, she had prepared for this interaction and already knew the answers to the questions she would ask.

'Yes, madam, please ask your question now,' said Biswas.

'Did Tagore get instant recognition as an artist in India?' asked Patty.

'Interesting that you should ask. Actually, he did not,' replied Biswas. 'During the early years of his life as an artist, he did not receive a warm reception from his countrymen. He was disappointed and decided not to exhibit his artwork in India. His artwork, however, was received with much delight and excitement abroad, resulting in multiple exhibitions.

'In the spring of 1930, while on a tour to France, he was advised by some art critics from local newspapers who had seen his paintings, to hold an exhibition in Paris. Accordingly, he held the first public exhibition of his paintings in Paris in May 1930, at the Gallerie Pigalle. Duchess Anna de Noailles, in her introductory remarks described her experience of it: "To me it is like climbing a staircase of dreamland."

'After the conclusion of the exhibition at Paris, similar exhibitions were held in England, Denmark, Sweden, Rome, Germany and Russia. Later, exhibitions were also held in the USA and Canada.

'The international audience recognised the strength and style of Tagore's paintings and welcomed them with immense praise. Tagore was exhilarated and wrote to his son Rathindranath in 1930: "From my experience of my painting exhibitions in Europe I realise I can rely on my ability of painting." In 1930 he also wrote to Pratimadevi, his daughter-in-law, saying, "My paintings command decent prices which will increase in the coming years." Tagore was immensely pleased when the Berlin National Gallery procured five of his paintings, and they were described with praise by newspapers in Europe and North America.

'After he had won accolades abroad, local critics started taking interest in his paintings and an exhibition was organised in Kolkata in 1932 by Mukul Dey, an ex-student of Shantiniketan and the principal of the Government College of Art, Kolkata.'

'I hope I have answered your question,' said Biswas.

'Yes, Mr Mukherjee,' replied Patty. 'It is intriguing that even someone with the stature of Tagore found it difficult to establish himself as an artist in India.'

'Yes, you are right,' replied Biswas. 'There is no easy path to becoming an artist. The rules are the same whether in India or abroad, it doesn't matter whether you are Van Gogh or Rabindranath Tagore.'

'Any more questions, Yes, sir, you at the back.'

'Can you tell us about Tagore's views on education?'

'Tagore was far ahead of his time when it came to creating an education system. He wanted to bring the learning from his family upbringing to his school at Shantiniketan. He had envisioned an education system that was deeply influenced by one's immediate surroundings but associated with the cultures of the wider world, grounded upon pleasurable learning and customised to the personality of the child. His views are best described in the following paragraph from one of his books:

"We have come to this world to accept it, not merely

to know it. We may become powerful by knowledge but we attain fullness by sympathy. The highest education is that which does not merely give us information but makes our life in harmony with all existence. But we find that this education of sympathy is not only systematically ignored in schools, it is severely repressed. We rob the child of his earth to teach him geography, of language to teach him grammar. His hunger is for the epic, but he is supplied with chronicles of facts and dates…Child-nature protests against such calamity with all its power of suffering, subdued at last into silence by punishment.'"

'What role did Tagore play in the development of art and culture?' asked someone in the back row.

'Tagore's involvement with art and culture preceded his development as an artist. While the first doodles in Purabi appeared in 1924, marking the beginning of his artistic career, his stature as a Nobel Laureate and public intellectual ensured that he had been involved in contemporary debates on art and culture early on. While he encouraged the resurgence of Indian art, he warned his nephew Abindranath, who led the Bengal School, of the futility of moving away from western academic arts only to be drawn to ancient Indian traditions. The idea of cultural nationalism was driving them towards historicism but Tagore believed that they should be influenced by their Asian roots at large and even more importantly, by life around them.

'When he travelled to Japan in 1916, Tagore found that Japanese art was sensitive to nature and monumental in scope. Its design added beauty to every aspect of life and it was woven into the social fabric. He was very impressed and wrote letters to his nephews recording his realisations.

'Sensing that only his personal involvement would ensure the fruition of these plans, he set up the Kala Bhavan at Shantiniketan to promote art under the leadership of Nandalal Bose. Tagore had clear ideas about the pedagogy of art; Nandalal was an able lieutenant who gave shape to his ideas.'

Biswas was now looking at his watch. This Q&A session was taking too long and he was getting annoyed. He announced, 'One last question before I leave.'

'Mr Mukherjee, can you please shed some light on your research work at Shantiniketan,' asked Patty.

He smiled. He was hoping someone would ask him about his accomplishments in the field of art history and research. Patty knew she had nailed it. What followed was a long discussion about his life as a scholar.

'I don't know where to begin,' he said. 'But let me try.'

'After passing out of the JJ School of Art with honours, I spent close to a decade trying to find inner peace by doing various odd jobs in art and related fields in Mumbai and Kolkata before finally arriving at Shantiniketan, the abode of learning created by Tagore. I was mesmerised by the environment of Shantiniketan and finally felt at peace with myself there.

'If you have been to Shantiniketan, you would know that it consists of two wings, Viswa Bharati, the University and Kala Bhavan, the School of Art and Culture. I volunteered as a junior research associate at Kala Bhavan. While the salary was meagre and hardly sufficient to meet my daily expenses, I had finally found a platform and environment of learning which could be exploited to satisfy my inner hunger for knowledge. I immersed myself in researching the life of the old masters like Rabindranath Tagore, Jamini Roy and Nandalal Bose.

'My work was almost immediately rewarded by one of the professors at the institution who was writing a comprehensive research paper on the oeuvre of Rabindranath Tagore. The professor was very impressed with my knowledge of the artist and took me under his wing as a scholar. The paper required a lot of travel to various institutions across the country to conduct research and study Tagore's art. Since I was representing Shantiniketan, I was granted unhindered access to libraries, archives, museums, galleries and private collections. Thus, began my infatuation with the works of Tagore.

'During the course of my innumerable visits to galleries and private exhibitions, I realised that a lack of proper documentation was a significant problem plaguing a large portion of Tagore's paintings that were held by private collectors and galleries. Very few paintings could be linked back to the Grand Master. Due to a lack of documentation and research, there were paintings with questionable provenance being attributed to Tagore, on the one hand, while on the other, there were paintings which were created in his style, in his blood and flesh which still cried out to be discovered. I made detailed notes of my findings and presented the same to my professor for evaluation.

'After my submission, Shantiniketan re-evaluated its existing process of art authentication and attribution. A few paintings which had earlier been attributed to Tagore were dropped from the catalogue, while a dozen new paintings were re-evaluated. Almost 80 per cent of the documented paintings were subsequently accepted as new findings of the artist and his existing oeuvre was accordingly expanded. This highlights the fact that the existing art infrastructure in India is weak, insufficient and incomplete and in need of urgent research work.

'After assisting the professor, I continued my scholarly work at Shantiniketan over the next decade, writing several papers on the evolution and development of the Bengal School. These were much appreciated in the art fraternity and published in different art journals and papers. Gradually, I began to be recognised in the art circles as an expert on the Bengal School and was often consulted by galleries, museums and collectors for my views and assistance in different matters relating to the evolution of art and the impact of the Bengal School.'

As he ended his speech, he had a broad smile on his face. The audience looked tired, except for Patty who appeared inquisitive. She anxiously waited for him to come down from the dais to make her next move.

≈

Chapter 7

The Fading Star

When Arun finally emerged from the attic after what seemed an eternity, he looked different. He was much thinner and sported a long dark beard. He was satisfied with the quality of his masterpieces, a few dozen of them created in the style of the Grand Master.

However, creating quality forgeries was only the first step in becoming a master art forger. You had to successfully sell the paintings and this was no easy task. You needed an entire village to sell a forgery, to create the provenance necessary to ensure that the painting could be passed off as a genuine creation of the master. But he had no such luck on his side. He was on his own, he couldn't trust anyone, not even his own family. It had to be done discreetly and required meticulous planning and execution. He needed to be sober and that was much easier said than done.

There were two factors working in his favour. These could help him create a plausible story. Perhaps not the most perfect, but something that could not be ignored. This was all he needed, given the exceptional quality of his masterpieces. Like the Grand Master's, his family too, belonged to Bengal and, more importantly, his grandfather had been an artist, a street painter in Kolkata in the early half of the twentieth century. This was the time when the Bengal movement had been taking shape under the leadership of Tagore's nephew, Abindranath.

Arun had listened to his father narrate stories about his grandfather and his immediate peer group of artists, many of whom had been active in the Bengal movement and belonged to the Government College of Arts, Kolkata and Kala Bhavan at Shantiniketan. The fact that none of them was a distinguished artist didn't matter. If he could somehow weave a story around that background and corroborate it, it would be difficult for an average person to deny the possibility that he could have come into possession of a painting by the Grand Master.

There had to be some material in the house, some old photographs, memorabilia or perhaps a diary. Over the next week, he turned his house upside down, looking through old family albums, participation certificates, awards, posters, any other evidence that could link him to early twentieth-century Kolkata and corroborate his grandfather's background as a street painter. At the end of this exercise, he had managed to collect several pieces of evidence, none of which were important on their own but put together, told a plausible story.

He had now in his possession a few photographs from the 1920s and early 1930s that showed his grandfather posing in front of theatre collages and advertisements in several recognisable monuments in Kolkata. In one of the photographs, his grandfather was eating food in a canteen with several people, the Government College of Arts clearly visible in the background. He also found original hand-painted posters of some popular theatres in Kolkata, including a few circus performances with visible dates. He created a scrapbook with all this material arranged in chronological order. Now that the evidence to explain the provenance had been organised, the next step was to identify a gallery to buy his painting.

He knew how the galleries in Mumbai and in the other big cities worked. He had tried unsuccessfully to put up his paintings in some of them in the past. They never bought on impulse and in cash. All purchases were on credit with payments being received over a few weeks. It wasn't that they didn't have the money to pay. They used this credit period to have the paintings carefully evaluated and authenticated by their in-house experts. Payments were made only once the evaluation was satisfactory. Further, most of them dealt only with well-established clients with whom they had a history of transactions. In case of a new client, they required references. Purchases were made only once the references had been confirmed. Further, he risked being identified at a few of these galleries.

For his plan to succeed, he needed a gallery which made on-the-spot payments in cash, a gallery which was small and discreet, that wouldn't subject him to too many questions. Perhaps a proprietary concern. The sale had to be a one-off event because he didn't want to leave any evidence that could be traced back to him. He decided to focus his attention on category B towns in India which were high on the art scene, such as Nagpur, Baroda, Ahmedabad, Hyderabad and Gwalior. It was much safer to approach the smaller galleries that dotted these towns. These galleries were not equipped to deal with a high-quality forgery.

The first city he visited was Baroda, which had developed as a centre of art and culture. He spent the first few days visiting the different galleries that dotted the city. On the third day, he finally found a gallery to his liking, discreet and small, located in a bylane. He sat in an eatery, sipping tea and observing this gallery. The signage was dilapidated, a few characters missing from the name. In the hour that he sat at the eatery, not a single customer entered the gallery. He wasn't surprised. It looked uninviting, and any passer-by would have given it a miss. But for him it was the perfect gallery. He wanted a dark and dingy place located in some obscure bylane where he was unlikely to be disturbed while delivering his well-rehearsed sales pitch.

The next day, when the city was quieter after lunch, he reached the gallery, the painting securely tucked under his arm. He was amused to see that the security guard at the entrance, despite his uncomfortable seat, was dozing off in the mid-afternoon sun, sweat dripping from his eyebrows. He softly nudged his shoulder, waking him from his deep slumber into sudden attention.

'Is there anyone inside the gallery? The lights don't seem to be on.'

The guard pulled out his water flask, threw some water on his handkerchief and wiped his hot sweaty face with it.

He drank some water and then slowly turned his eyes in his direction, examining the figure standing in front of him. Looking disinterested and upset on being woken from his mid-afternoon nap, he said, 'Sethji is resting inside; that's why the lights are turned off.'

'I wish to meet with him.'

Glancing at the frame under his arms, the security guard slowly opened the door to the gallery and beckoned him inside, shouting over his shoulders, 'Sethji, there is a customer.'

Arun entered the gallery, where it took him a few seconds to get accustomed to the darkness. He could faintly see a man whom he presumed to be the owner sitting behind a desk at one end of the room. The man reached out to turn on the light behind him. Suddenly the room was illuminated; a broken chandelier with a few missing bulbs and walls with broken plaster urgently crying for a new coat of paint swam before his eyes. There were frames lying all over the room, piled on top of one another and almost reaching the ceiling. They were covered with an inch of dirt and cobwebs.

The only part in the room that was clean and appeared to be regularly dusted was the desk. Behind it sat a middle-aged, balding man who was gazing in his direction with piercing eyes, trying to decipher this customer dressed in simple trousers which despite the many rounds of alteration still didn't fit well and an untucked shirt, sweat marks clearly visible in the underarms.

Arun had specifically dressed so that he didn't stand out and looked like any other person on the streets of India.

'What do you want?'

'Sethji, I need some money for a family emergency. I was hoping to pawn my family's heirloom, a painting which has been with our family since well before my birth.'

Looking him in the eye, the owner yelled, 'This is an art gallery which buys and sells paintings, not a pawn shop.'

Arun made a desperate plea but the gallery owner stood his ground.

'Don't get upset, let me see what is it that you carry. Since you have come all this way, I will give you a free appraisal of the painting. Maybe you will change your mind.' He switched on another light and asked Arun to lay the painting on the desk. 'Come on, don't worry; you can always walk out of the gallery without doing the deal.'

Arun hesitantly removed the cloth covering the painting and placed it on the desk. As the light illuminated the wild brush strokes, highlighting the figure of the heavily veiled woman with a melancholy expression, the gallery owner nearly fell off his chair. He took a few moments to recompose himself. He immediately recognised the portrait of a heavily veiled woman as one of the masterpieces by Guru Rabindranath Tagore. Such a painting had never come into his gallery before.

Arun saw the rising excitement and the suspicion in the eyes of the gallery owner. As expected, the owner asked him, 'Do you know how your family came to possess this painting?'

'Sir, my family belongs to Bengal. This painting was gifted by a friend to my grandfather who was a well-known street artist in Kolkata. My father once told me that this person was an ardent collector and follower of the Bengal School.'

'Do you have any proof?'

'No sir, I don't have any receipt of purchase. As I mentioned earlier, this was a gift from a family friend.'

'I don't want a receipt; give me any evidence that helps to corroborate your story about how the painting came in your possession.'

'Sir, I have a few photographs of my grandfather and some of his works. However, I don't know if they are sufficient to calm your suspicions.'

'Where are they? Show them to me.'

Arun slowly pulled out the scrapbook from the cloth bag hung over his shoulders.

'This poster was painted by my grandfather,' he excitedly explained to the gallery owner, running him through a few of the original posters in the scrapbook.

The owner closely examined the scrapbook, asking him questions about the photographs while glancing at the portrait of the woman that lay in front of him.

Arun highlighted the photograph that showed his grandfather in the canteen of the Government College of Art, sharing his lunch with a few other artists. He pointed out a figure in the photograph. 'Sir, look at this gentleman here; he is the one who had gifted the painting to my grandfather. He used to study in the Government College of Art when Mr Mukul Dey was the principal of the college. My grandfather had done some pro bono work for this gentleman; this painting was a gift, a gesture of friendship.'

The owner suddenly yelled for the security guard. He got no response. 'Bastard, have you gone off to sleep again? How can you sleep on that broken three-legged stool that I have provided you?'

Arun's heart skipped a beat. 'Has he got wind of my scam?' he wondered. He looked anxiously behind him at the front gate, waiting for the guard to appear. The wait seemed to be never-ending; there were beads of sweat running down his forehead.

The guard suddenly appeared. 'Close the gallery. I am taking care of some important business and am not to be disturbed,' the owner yelled, much to Arun's relief.

'Where have you all disappeared? Get a cup of tea for the customer!' he called to the servant. Then looking at Arun, he said, 'You are feeling hot and here I am ordering tea. I am so sorry, sir. Cancel the tea and get some lemon water instead,' he called out again.

He suddenly looked Arun in the eye and asked, 'Do you know the relevance and importance of this painting?'

'Sir, my father had once mentioned that this was an important piece of work by Rabindranath Tagore; however, I don't know its relevance. I have seen it since my childhood, hanging in the living room and collecting dust.'

'Your father told you right. We are looking at a masterpiece by Guru Rabindranath Tagore. The portrait of a veiled woman was a theme that he was obsessed with and revisited many times in his career. In fact, I had seen an article a few months ago in one of the magazines that had a few photos of paintings by the Grand Master. Let me see if I can find it.'

The owner told the servant to ensure Arun was comfortable as he disappeared inside. Arun could see him frantically fiddling through a bunch of books, dust flying all over the room. He appeared with an old magazine in his hands. Arun looked on in disgust as the owner blew hot air from his mouth over the magazine cover and a pile of dust flew in the air. 'I am sorry it is a little dirty,' he said. Flipping through the magazine, he found the relevant article and pointed to an illustration of a portrait of a woman that had been created by Tagore.

The magazine described the painting in detail, the uneven brush movements, the heavy veil, the darkness against the bright background, the melancholy features of the face. It mentioned that Tagore had created various versions of this portrait over the last two decades of his life. The gallery owner carefully examined the painting and described the similarities to the illustration in his hand. With every similarity, his excitement increased exponentially. It was almost as if he had become a boy full of energy and life.

Arun could see the rising excitement in the eyes of the owner, his uncontrollable greed. He knew that the owner was sold on the painting and would not allow him to leave the gallery without purchasing it. Before he could ask him any further questions on his family background or the provenance of the painting, Arun said, 'Sir, will you allow me to pawn this painting? I had mentioned to you earlier that this is my family heirloom and I will not be able to part with it.'

These words came as a jolt to the owner. He had already presumed that the painting was his to keep.

The roles had been reversed. It was now the owner who had to convince Arun why he should part with the painting. All doubts and questions he had regarding the provenance of the painting a few moments earlier were no longer relevant, quietly buried in the background, never to come up again during the course of the discussion.

'Think of what you can do with all this money,' the owner yelled, pushing forty crisp 100-rupee notes in Arun's hand.

Thereafter, he anxiously examined the expression on Arun's face.

Even before Arun could react, the owner yelled, 'Not enough? No problem. Here, take ten more,' as he pushed another 1000 rupees in Arun's hand and closed his fist.

Arun looked at the 5000 rupees in his hand. This was more money than he had ever seen at one time in his life. This was more than the income that he had earned the previous year, working at the frame and restoration shop.

Even before he could revel in the moment, the owner thanked him for accepting the offer and personally walked him out of the main door of the gallery. No sooner had Arun ventured outside the gallery than he could hear the shutters close behind him.

Over the next five years, he travelled to different parts of the country, visiting small art galleries and selling several dozen artworks supposedly created by Tagore. He used the same modus operandi as before—visiting small galleries in the mid-afternoon when general traffic was low, catching the gallery owners off guard with his offer to pawn his family heirloom and thereafter, walking out with money after showing much disinterest in selling the artwork. He always ensured that his attire was that of a simple man who could easily blend in with the crowds. His act worked time and again because he had a story which could partly explain the provenance of the artwork, given his family's artistic and geographical background. After telling it, he depended on the sheer greed of the gallery owners to overcome their initial caution and suspicion. He enjoyed watching them convince themselves of the once-in-a lifetime opportunity that had walked into their gallery, a person with limited knowledge of art holding a masterpiece which could be sold for a hefty profit. The results were always the same. The owners ensured that there was urgency in the sale, so Arun wouldn't have time to reflect upon his decision. In their hurry to conclude the sale, they never asked him difficult questions such as the provenance of the painting or his contact address. The sale was immediate, in cash and without a receipt. This worked perfectly well for Arun, who walked out of the gallery with cash in hand, the quantum of which increased with every successive visit to a new gallery.

For his part, Arun ensured that he never visited the same gallery twice. He knew that his plan worked because he gave the impression that it was a one-off sale and he had walked into the gallery by chance. If he went back to the same gallery with another painting of the master, then it would raise much suspicion and nervousness in the minds of the gallery owners, resulting in intense questioning. He played his role perfectly, never showing urgency, remaining calm and composed.

Unknown to Arun, the small galleries acted as collection centres for the larger galleries in the big cities of Mumbai and Delhi. Dealers visited these smaller galleries regularly, looking for new finds which could be flipped for a profit after a mark-up. Within a short period of time, all the forgeries had found their way to the larger galleries of Delhi, Mumbai and Kolkata. In the process, they had passed through various intermediaries and smaller galleries, been showcased at different exhibitions and thus created the necessary documentary trail in terms of bills and invoices, documentation in catalogues and listings in exhibitions, which were necessary to create provenance.

By the beginning of 1970, Arun had acquired significant wealth by selling a few dozen paintings. These forgeries adorned the walls of some of the most respectable institutions in the art world. He was amazed by the reviews that some of them received at exhibitions held by art experts and curators of well-known galleries and art connoisseurs alike.

This false glory misled him into believing that times had changed and encouraged him to once again take a leap of faith and try his hand at becoming an artist. Accordingly, he produced a series of works under his own name and used his financial clout to have them placed at some of the leading galleries in Mumbai. However, whatever self-belief he had was soon shattered as none of his paintings found a buyer. He couldn't understand what was happening. Why were people falling all over each other to buy his art when it carried the signature of the Grand Master but there were no takers for the same under his own name? Were people buying art for its aesthetic beauty or merely paying for the signature of the Grand Master?

This dilemma forced him into a state of depression. What should he do next? It was easy for him to go back into the world of art forgery and make a living, but in his heart he was a true artist and despised the thought of creating paintings in styles and themes that were alien to him in order to please the art world. Earlier, he had felt righteous in his pursuit of art forgery, driven by his hatred and frustration of the art world that had denied him his basic artistic existence. However, even in those days he needed the support of intoxicants to overcome his inhibitions and internal conflicts while creating forgeries of the Grand Master. Every time he woke up in the morning, the influence of the intoxicant waning, he had felt a sinking feeling in his stomach, telling him that all was not well.

As time passed, art forgery had become the means of his livelihood, offering him money and wealth to afford luxuries. It was no longer a weapon bestowed upon him to fight the injustices of the art world. He could no longer morally justify his nightly pursuits towards financial fulfilment and had started disliking the same. He felt a strong sense of guilt in his mind, knowing well that had his father been alive, he would have never concurred with his choice to lead the life of an art forger. It was because of this that he had made fresh attempts at becoming an artist. However, that art world didn't seem ready to give him the chance.

Frustrated, depressed and with no one to guide him or speak to him, he fell back on the only friend he had in moments of darkness, alcohol. He would drink from dawn till dusk, always intoxicated and locked in constant battle with the demons inside his mind. He would speak to himself, recite the poems of Tagore or dream about Kadambari Devi. His mother and sister, concerned that he was becoming a lunatic, decided to send him to a rehabilitation centre. The spark in his eyes gradually faded a person of raw artistic talent lost the battle to become a successful contemporary artist for his time.

Chapter 8

Method in Madness

As Biswas walked down the dais, he was surrounded by the participants of the seminar. Patty stood at a distance waiting for the initial euphoria to settle and the crowds to disperse. Once Biswas was alone, she approached him.

'Mr Mukherjee, it is an honour to finally meet you in person. You might not know who I am, but I have been an ardent follower and admirer of your research work. That last article you wrote in the art journal on the ever present jivanadevata in Tagore's life and works was truly path breaking.'

'Thank you for your kind words,' replied Biswas, now sporting a wide smile. 'I could see your enthusiasm when I was making the speech. What is your name?'

'Patty, sir.'

'So Patty, what do you do for a living?'

'I own an art gallery, sir,' she replied. 'Actually, I own two of them.'

There was a sudden change in Biswas's body language.

The smile had disappeared and his arms were now folded around his chest.

He was generally cautious when meeting dealers and gallery owners, those he held responsible for the commercialisation and degeneration of the art world. He had found them to be hollow with little or no substance, a complete waste of time. Such people annoyed him. But she was different.

'What is it, madam?' he asked, his words a little terse.

She could see that he was uncomfortable and she had to act fast.

'Sir, I can see the sudden change in your body language. Frankly, I don't blame you. The reputation of art dealers and gallery owners is much maligned. All I can say in my defence is that I am not like them.'

Her words had an immediate impact on him. His arms, which had been folded only a minute earlier, were now in his pockets and he appeared more relaxed and open.

'I can see that,' he replied with a smile. 'That's why we are still having this conversation.'

Patty knew how to handle people like him; they represented a different breed, stuck in a time warp, passionately engrossed in their research while completely oblivious to the changes in society and the industry around them. The only way to cut through their defences and to reach out to them was to do your homework and admire their work.

'Sir, I have two art galleries in India,' Patty continued, reeling him in. 'One in Mumbai and another in Delhi. They have grown in size and stature over the last decade and are in urgent need of a curator. I need someone with a deep knowledge and understanding of Indian art, with the dedication and commitment to carry the candle to unravel the darkness and mysteries of the art industry.'

'Madam, I am a research scholar. My work is recognized in the old world. I am a misfit in the art industry to which you belong,' Biswas said.

She smiled. 'Don't worry, sir. I understand your inhibitions. You will have complete autonomy in your research assignments. All I ask is that you assist us in identifying emerging trends and new artists.'

Biswas promised to get back to her.

He was surprised by his own reply. It wasn't something he had said in passing to get this aggressive and persuasive woman off his back. He was actually intrigued by the unexpected offer and was considering it. He was cautious as he knew all too well that these art industry people were not to be trusted; all they ever wanted was money. However, at the same time, he couldn't help but be excited. A curatorial job at a leading art gallery with a presence in Delhi and Mumbai, the latter the mecca of the modern art scene in India, would give him access to a much larger platform on which he could showcase his research.

The woman, Patty or whatever her name was, had sounded sincere. For once he had met a gallery owner with some substance, someone who wasn't merely faffing in the air.

Also, Shantiniketan had become drab by now, too slow and bureaucratic. It was no longer the institution of learning and cutting-edge research that he had joined over a decade earlier. He often felt suffocated and confined in its environment. There was so much more that he wished to do. He had started rebelling but they were too slow in their reactions and even when they did react, their responses were very measured. In contrast, the art world was changing at a rapid pace and needed the erstwhile institution, which had once defined its very parameters, to play a more active role.

After a few days of deliberation, influenced of course, by Patty's relentless follow-up, he decided to accept her offer on the condition that there would be no intervention in his academic and research pursuits and that the gallery would sponsor and assist him in authoring the Catalogue Raisonné of Rabindranath Tagore. While making this decision, he had discounted, perhaps out of sheer excitement, the fact that a curatorial job involved operational and commercial duties which were not to his liking. Further, while he would have the opportunity to interact with known collectors and connoisseurs, there would be an underlying pressure to convert these meetings into commercial successes. The constant pressure of sales and marketing would come to haunt him in the future.

Within a few months of taking on his new assignment, he requested Patty to set up a marathon meeting to chalk out the strategy of the gallery. At this meeting, he impressed upon her the need to allow him to commence work on the creation of the Catalogue Raisonné. Besides being a branding exercise which would bring the gallery much publicity and acknowledgement, launching it into a new sphere, the Catalogue was the perfect front to gain vital information about the location and ownership of rare pieces of art of the old masters, the Navaratnas, which lay scattered in the nooks and corners of the country. He thought that the Navaratnas could be the next big trend in the art industry. While once highly sought, they were now available at a deep discount in comparison to their intrinsic value. If a gallery could acquire and successfully market them, the opportunities were immense. Patty was impressed by the plan and asked him to commence work on the Catalogue while she simultaneously worked in the background, aggregating works of the old masters.

Over the course of his research work at Shantiniketan, Biswas had realised that there were a lot of gaps in the documented oeuvre of Tagore. Even with the meagre budget that had been allocated to him for the research paper, he had successfully identified almost a dozen paintings whose existence was not reflected in the existing archives. Now, with a much larger budget at his disposal together with the recognition he had earned as a leading art expert and scholar, he felt that he had the opportunity once and for all to comprehensively document the works of Tagore and give the old master the respect that he deserved.

He focused his research on four specific areas: the artwork itself, provenance, exhibition and literature. He exploited his contacts in the art industry to reach out to every known museum, art gallery, dealer or collector who was known to have dealt in the works of Tagore. This also involved regular interaction and travel abroad, thanks to Tagore's celebrity status and visits to Europe and North America.

Given his past work on Tagore and comparatively easy access, it took him only six years to complete the Catalogue

Raisonné. The Catalogue was a scholarly undertaking, an analytical or 'reasoned' compilation of all the known works of Tagore. Its objective was to present the full breadth of Tagore's accomplishment, comprehensively, with nothing left out. The works were arranged in chronological order, with entries on each work listing its dimensions, the materials used in its creation, every exhibition it had been showcased in, every book and article in which it had been mentioned and all that was known about its provenance.

In preparing the Catalogue, Biswas evaluated the artworks on connoisseurship and a close visual analysis of the work to determine whether it looked and 'felt' like a work by Tagore. He paid special attention to composition, brushstroke, colour, surface and the signature, if there was one.

He delved into the provenance, trying to reconstruct the ownership history of the work from the time it was said to have left Tagore's studio. This was the most difficult part of the job, as complete ownership history was seldom available in India where sales were often in cash and seldom recorded. The art market was notoriously opaque and not all owners were forthcoming about when and where they had obtained their pieces. Even people who had nothing to hide were often reluctant to have their names published as owners.

He looked into the historical context, evaluated the style of the work and compared it to other works by Tagore done around the time the one in question was supposed to have been created. An artist's style changed over his lifetime, reaching a zenith and subsequently declining.

Working on the Catalogue was very intriguing. At one

end were connoisseurs and collectors who did not wish to be identified as owners of known works of Tagore and consequently refused to grant access to their collections. On the other, there were those who approached him through references, requesting him to include works supposedly by Tagore. These had dodgy provenance and even dodgier brush movements. Contrary to his solitary work in the past, the art fraternity was suddenly interested in what was included and excluded from Biswas's Catalogue. Inclusion of a work in the Catalogue Raisonné greatly strengthened its provenance and, consequently, its financial value. Likewise, a work which was excluded raised doubts about its provenance and authenticity, thereby decimating its value.

For the first time, Biswas found himself the focus of a lot of attention, his every action examined by the art fraternity. This was his first true interaction with commercialisation in the art world.

However, true to his research ethics, he stood his ground and ensured that every work presented to him for inclusion was subjected to the same degree of diligence and rigour. Though it was possible that due to lack of information and availability, some works might have been excluded from the catalogue, he could proudly declare that no incorrect work had found place in it.

In a few cases where known works could not be located, either because they were feared to have been destroyed by the passage of time or because the current owners did not identify themselves, Biswas wrote about these works on the basis of recollections from exhibitions, literature and past owners. It was specifically mentioned in the Catalogue that these works had not been personally evaluated due to a lack of availability; however, they had a recorded history of ownership.

Chapter 9

Successful Artists Live Long—Perhaps Too Long

Jay's career in the capital markets was over. He had been both humiliated and disgraced, banned from accessing and dealing in securities for five years. In order to contain the damage, his erstwhile employer had fired him while simultaneously feigning ignorance before the regulators. He was persona non grata in the capital market industry.

He had used the past few weeks to introspect. To try and understand how things had gone so horribly wrong. Only a few weeks earlier he was unstoppable, the shining star consistently breathing down Samir's neck for the number two position in the organisation. And now, he was without a job. However, blinded by his overconfidence, he refused to delve into the questions that actually needed answering. For example, did he perform comprehensive diligence before accepting the assignment? If he did, then how come he did not know about the estranged brother? Putting the blame on the client was a lame excuse. Clients never spoke the truth and if they did, then diligence wouldn't be needed, would it? He should have known that something was amiss, it seemed too damn easy. In his overconfidence, he had overruled the reservations raised by Samir, calling him an ageing man who was fast losing his appetite for taking risks.

Hence, when the shit hit the fan, he wasn't upset by the behaviour of his ex-employer. He could understand it: he had become a liability and was no longer useful. Had he been in Samir's position, he would have probably done the same. However, he was extremely upset with the behaviour of the regulators. They appeared to be on a personal vendetta, making an example out of him. They went about thumping their chests and drawing a media frenzy. The corresponding coverage had tarnished his reputation in the market and humiliated him.

But for the last few weeks, he had had a fabulous innings at his job, creating substantial wealth for himself and he was now on the lookout for a new business opportunity, a new idea where he could deploy his money to generate wealth. Actually, more than the wealth he wanted to earn back the respect and reputation that he had lost at the hands of the regulators.

He needed to re-engage with his social circle which, despite his best intentions, had been neglected for the past few months due to his huge workload.

When he entered the venue of the dinner party organised by a leading industrialist, he was immediately aware of the piercing gaze that followed him wherever he went. He was used to getting attention from women; however, whenever he tried making eye contact with them, they usually looked the other way. This woman was different. He had looked into her eyes on two separate occasions and she hadn't even flinched or batted an eyelid, making him, usually so sure of himself, feel uncomfortable. She was standing at the centre of a group of middle-aged men and engaging in a conversation, the men listening intently to what she had to say. Intrigued by her aggressive behaviour, he decided to learn more about her.

As he came closer, he realised that most of the men in the group though pretending to listen to her pearls of wisdom were actually gazing at her cleavage, perhaps hoping to catch a glimpse of what was hidden while enjoying what was already on offer. Further, it was apparent that the lady at the centre was not oblivious to this attention; in fact, she seemed to be enjoying it.

'Hello. I don't believe we've met? My name is Jay Malhotra,' he said.

'I'm Priya Chawla,' she smiled. 'My friends call me Patty.'

It was difficult to ascertain her age. She was definitely older than he was but by how many years he couldn't tell. One thing was certain, she had spent considerable time, effort and money to look the way she did. She wore a black Valentino evening gown and it was obvious she was the star of the evening. Her body was in perfect proportion; her well-toned arms and the faint outline of her curvaceous derriere suggested that she spent several hours in the gym every week.

He joined the group and unlike many others around him actually listened intently to the discussion at hand.

'Oh, I am sorry, Mr Meswani, but the Raza was sold last week. You were the first port of call. I warned you that there was phenomenal interest so you should have closed the sale immediately. But you dilly-dallied for far too long. No harm done, I am likely to get another one this month of even better provenance. Though, I must warn you, it will be expensive. Just make sure you move faster this time.'

Another person suddenly spoke out from the group...

'Hey, Patty! Remember that artist you mentioned last month who ate a kilogram of meat in front of you?'

'Yeah! What about him?'

'I bought two of his paintings.'

'Okay. But why?' she asked.

'I figured that given his age, you mentioned late eighties and his diet, he wouldn't live for long.'

She smiled as she faced the gentleman.

'I guess I forgot to mention that he has been eating that diet for the past ten years I have known him,' she replied. 'Also, he doesn't seem to have aged a year in that period. Next time seek professional advice before making these decisions,' she laughed.

All the others laughed in chorus along with her.

It seemed like Patty was an art dealer and was in the midst of a very well-rehearsed and effective sales pitch. The group of men surrounding her were suckers who had either bought paintings from her in the past or were prospective clients.

'She is really good,' he thought. 'Her sales pitch is impeccable.'

Suddenly, Patty looked at him.

'So Mr Malhotra, what is it that you do?'

'I am between jobs right now. I'm trying to figure out

what to do next.'

There was an immediate sparkle in Patty's eyes; maybe she had found her sucker for the night. She left the group on the pretext of getting some fresh air and winked at Jay to follow her. Jay responded by picking up two glasses of champagne and moving onto the patio.

'That was a brilliant sales pitch that you made back there, truly commendable. I am sure that Meswani fellow will be wagging his tail to your gallery in no time.'

'Oh, so you noticed. Am I supposed to be flattered? Was that a compliment?'

'Yes, of course, I choose my words very carefully, seldom giving compliments.'

Patty realised that he was no sucker but since she found him interesting, she decided to keep talking to him anyway.

'So, are you going to buy any of the paintings?'

'No, I am not. You must have figured that out by now. I was hoping that wasn't the only reason you pulled me to the patio. After all, I couldn't help but notice that you have been looking at me ever since I entered the party.'

'Nothing seems to escape your eyes, Mr Malhotra. May I call you Jay?'

'Yes, you may. So Patty, tell me more about your art industry. Does it have more interesting people like you?'

'There is no dearth of people, but there is only one Patty,' she replied.

For the next two hours, Jay and Patty were engaged in a serious discussion about the dynamics of the art industry. He couldn't believe what he heard. The macros were too good to be true; the industry was totally unregulated, very new and growing at an exponential pace. Further, it was highly fragmented with no large dominant players. After several more glasses of champagne, their discussion was cut short by the sudden appearance of the host who informed them that food had been served. As Patty proceeded towards the dining area, she patted Jay on his bottom. 'I am travelling to Mashobra for a few weeks—why don't we meet again after that?' she asked with a smile.

'But I don't have your phone number!' he yelled.

'I am sure you will manage,' she said, and left.

As she left, Jay wondered if the art industry represented the opportunity that he had been searching for. Prima facie, the art industry checked all the boxes. It was virgin and growing, it was fragmented and most importantly it didn't have any regulators.

The art industry represented uncharted territory, much like a virgin in a crowded bar, waiting to be guided. With the backing of his high-networth clientele and business acumen, he could possibly dominate the art world to reclaim his position amongst the glitterati of the country. This opportunity was certainly worth exploring further and so was Patty, the art insider.

He hadn't met anyone like her before. Much like him, she knew what she wanted and was not scared to say it. He wanted to know what her story was, how she had transformed from Priya Chawla to Patty.

A few days later, he had found the answers to most of his questions. What he learnt appeared to be straight out of a

Bollywood movie. Patty hailed from Delhi. She was a widow who had been married to an industrialist. Her husband had committed suicide under mysterious circumstances. The moment he died, his house was swarming with creditors. Unknown to her, his business had not been doing well and he had borrowed heavily to fund his lavish lifestyle. Within a week, she had been thrown out of her house and her comfortable life became a distant dream. Her family deserted her in her hour of need, holding her responsible for her husband's death. Whether it was her demands that had driven him to his death, nobody could tell for certain, but there was enough fodder to keep the gossip mills busy for a few weeks.

Lonely and with nowhere to go, she turned to a few friends for help. She desperately needed a job to support herself but her lack of a college degree was a hindrance. Out of sympathy, one of her friends introduced her to a small gallery owner who was looking for people to sell paintings. Patty took the paintings on consignment and sold them on a commission basis to her friends and acquaintances from her kitty party circle. Initially, her friends bought them out of sheer sympathy, trying to help one of their own. However, she gradually became organised and started selling more expensive works at wine and cheese parties that she sponsored at the houses of her friends, thereby exploiting their social circles.

She did what was required to survive in an unforgiving world, exploiting her beauty and sexuality to her advantage. It was about survival in the beginning, but over a period of time it became a way of life for her, a path to success.

Her first gallery was born at Hauz Khas village in Delhi

in the late 1980s and as they say, the rest is history. Nothing succeeds like success. Today Patty was a well-known dealer who commanded respect in the art fraternity, ruthless in her business dealings as many rival galleries had realised too late to their own peril. Her clients included museums and some of the best-known art connoisseurs, collectors and industrialists. Her fancy could herald you to celebrity status overnight, her displeasure could throw you into oblivion. She was a go-getter, known to play dirty, break rules and do whatever was required to succeed.

She was also a known cougar, her interest in younger men well documented. Her past experiences had made her into the person she was today. When she was young and financially vulnerable, she had been exploited by many. Given, that she had spent a considerable part of her youth in building and creating the art business, she was now trying hard to catch up with lost time, doing whatever was required to look young. Also, now that she was strong, she was exploiting her position of dominance to date men who were much younger than her in age, who were financially and emotionally vulnerable like she had been many years earlier. She would ask them to move into her house, to enjoy her hospitality and in return she would seek sexual favours from them. They would go out together to parties and social events where she would walk proudly, displaying her latest acquisitions. She would be dependent on no one anymore.

Jay liked the idea of her preying on him. She would lead him on a good chase, given her experience. Maybe she could even teach him a thing or two about bedroom etiquette.

Chapter 10

Dr Gachet Screamed!

The global art world was transforming and evolving. Institutions which had once been its pillars of support were no longer suitable as the art world transitioned into an art industry. This transformation had replaced aesthetics, which used to be the sole criteria for buying an artwork, with economic considerations of value and marketability and had simultaneously accorded scientific technological methods of authentication an almost equal, if not higher, footing than traditional methods of connoisseurship.

Art had emerged as a new asset class estimated at over $50 billion annually, with hundreds of thousands of paintings and decorative works changing hands every year. It needed standardisation to promote marketability, transferability and scale. Consequently, art connoisseurship had been commodified.

The emergence of an art industry had led to an exponential growth in infrastructure, with thousands of galleries, dealers and experts cropping up overnight. The auction market had seen a stupendous growth from a mere $45 million in 1970 to $545 million in 1985 and $2.4 billion in 2000.

The motives behind buying art had also undergone a significant change. Earlier, direct consumption used to be the most important need that art helped to fulfil. This motive gradually changed in the early twentieth century to both direct and conspicuous consumption, that is, the signalling attributes of art—the prestige and signalling qualities enjoyed by collectors when they showcased the masterpieces in their possession to friends and acquaintances. However, direct consumption remained the dominant factor influencing purchase decisions. By the mid-1960s, investment as a motive for purchasing art had also started gaining importance.

But much had changed over the past three decades with art becoming an alternate asset class. While its aesthetic and signalling qualities still influenced decision-making, it was predominantly its investment value and forecasted future value that drove most purchase decisions now. A new breed of investors had emerged that dominated the art industry, advised by their private bankers and lawyers. They had limited knowledge and interest in the artworks they purchased, except as monetary investments for the future.

In the mid-1980s, when Andrea Mantegna's *Adoration of the Magi* sold for a whopping $10.4 million; it set a new world records auction price in for any work of art. This record was to be short-lived. In 1990, when Christopher Burge, the most successful auctioneer at Christie's sold Van Gogh's portrait of Dr Gachet in less than three minutes for $82.5 million, setting a new world record. There was sustained applause in the room for five full minutes. Burge later explained that he was disgusted and the applause was distasteful; that he had almost decided to walk out of the room as he realised that the applause was not for the work of art or for Van Gogh but for the power of money. Few would have thought that the record created that day would ever be broken. However, in 2012, Edvard Munch's *The Scream* sold for $119.9 million breaking all previous records. It is rumoured that private sales of major works have reached $250 million for a single painting. Such is the influence of greed and money in the art industry.

The art market in India has also been impacted by this rapid commercialisation and transformation into an industry. Prices of works of art by popular contemporary artists have increased over ten-fold in the past three decades. Numerous institutions of support have mushroomed across the country facilitating the buying and selling of works of art like galleries, dealers, experts, investors, collectors and auction houses. Art galleries are no longer institutions merely showcasing artists, but have taken a much wider role as advisors and trend-setters. Large galleries have built vast portfolios of different contemporary artists and are actively promoting them amongst investors.

According to various estimates, the art market in India is worth approximately $400 million. However, while small, it is one of the fastest growing markets in the world. This market is dominated by a few contemporary artists such as Souza, Raza, Husain, Mehta, Kumar and Gaitonde.

≋

Chapter 11

The Sexual Escapade

While the macros of the unregulated art world looked very promising, it was necessary for Jay to understand the micros, that is, the business dynamics of the art market, before he could take the plunge. The best way to gain this knowledge was to partner with an art insider. This would ensure that he didn't have to reinvent the wheel, saving him valuable time and preventing him from making the mistakes that are part of any learning process.

Who could be a better prospect for a business partner than Patty? She fit the description perfectly: an art insider who had risen through the ranks to run two of the most successful galleries in the country. Besides, she could be a lot of fun; he would dive into her arms, entice her with his money and body. He suddenly felt a bout of excitement, a feeling he had not experienced in the recent past.

The next day, he called Patty's gallery to find out about her whereabouts. The staff was noncommittal.

'Madam is not available, sir. She is currently on holiday.'

'I am aware of that, ma'dam, that's why I am asking you for her contact number.'

'I am sorry sir, but I am not at liberty to disclose her details.'

'Okay, listen. I don't have time to play musical chairs with you. I know Patty is in Mashobra, waiting anxiously for me to rendezvous with her. You can tell me where she is, in which case I will be much obliged. Otherwise you are certain to lose your job when she returns. And mind you, I will find out where she is in any case.'

After a moment's hesitation, he got his answer. Like he always did.

He immediately made his bookings at the same hotel and proceeded to Mashobra. Located at a height of 8000 feet on the old Hindustan–Tibet Road built by Lord Dalhousie in 1850, Mashobra was the summer retreat of the President of India. Despite being a mere 20 kilometres from the over-populated, polluted and brazen city of Shimla, it had retained its old-world charm and greenery and was surrounded by thick forests of pine, cedar, oak and horse chestnut.

He was heading to the old residence of Lord Kitchener, which had since been renovated and converted into a luxury hotel. As he drove through the lush green forests, in an SUV sent by the hotel to pick him up from the airport, his thoughts kept going to the arrangements he had made to make his stay comfortable and pleasurable. In all likelihood, Patty would have heard from her assistant that he was coming and would be expecting him, hence the element of surprise was no longer on his side. Despite this, he planned to make this encounter memorable. To this end, he had booked the finest suite at the hotel and bought a bottle of Dom Perignon to be kept by the bedside. He had requested the chef de cuisine to prepare tandoori trout for dinner, so freshly caught Kullu trout had been sourced for the evening. The table would be laid at the corner of the room, giving them much needed privacy. He had thereafter booked the jacuzzi located on the patio next to the indoor swimming pool. He planned to conclude his dinner by having his dessert and perhaps much more in the warmth of the jacuzzi, looking out upon the starry night.

Patty was delighted to see him and made no bones about it. She confessed at the dinner table that she had been confident of seeing him; she had left enough clues at the party to ensure he followed her to Mashobra. In fact, she would have been rather disappointed had he not taken the bait. They were merry in each other's company, giggling and enjoying the dinner. They were constantly flirting while holding hands but then suddenly Patty threw a spanner into the works.

'So Jay, I hear that they have banned you from the capital markets.'

The query took him by complete surprise and flipped him off his feet. Jay hadn't seen it coming. Perhaps that had reflected on his face.

'Oh! I am so sorry, Jay; I didn't intend to put you on the back foot. How uncouth of me. Here we were getting cosy, drinking champagne and silly me, I had to bring business into it.'

'No, no, it's absolutely fine, Patty.' He tried to compose

himself again. 'I intended to tell you about this later in the evening. I have been barred for a period of five years. I got caught on the wrong side of a trade with a few large institutions.'

He spent the next half hour casually discussing the facts with her, making it sound as though it wasn't a big deal, that somebody had to take the fall and unfortunately, it had been him. Patty played along and made him feel comfortable by sounding sympathetic.

'I know how these things are. They are always looking for a scapegoat in such circumstances.'

However, she wondered if Jay had been overly reckless—taking on large institutions could be suicidal. But she didn't let her inhibitions reflect on her face. She had her answers and it was time to steer the discussion away from his boring story.

'So Jay, what kind of women do you like?'

'I like women who are ambitious, aggressive and mischievous. Of course, they need to be attractive. Come to think of it, someone like you is perfectly my type. Patty, are you mischievous?'

'That is for you to find out.'

Their discussion grew more intimate, thanks to the constant eye contact and flowing champagne. Jay decided that the time had come to shift the action to the jacuzzi.

The jacuzzi was located next to the pool area, on the terrace of a secluded and private portion of the hotel. In the background, one could see the greater Himalayan ranges which looked silver now, their snow-capped peaks shining under the light of the full moon. The view to the left showed a ravine and the right was covered with thick forests of pine and oak. While the outside temperature was a chilly 2 degree Celsius, the water in the jacuzzi was maintained at a warm 38 degrees. As the cool air hit the warm water's surface, there was a constant generation of steam, which gave it a mystifying effect. When they arrived at the jacuzzi, Jay holding a bottle of champagne, their pretence could no longer hide their inner passion and the discussion quickly progressed from verbal to carnal pleasures. Patty ripped his shirt open, pulling on his trousers, wrapping her legs around his well-toned washboard stomach and holding on to his broad shoulders. Jay, in turn, groped her well-toned hips while continuously kissing her lips and moving further down her body. Soon, the moans of passion could no longer be subdued by the noise of the gushing water. It was almost as if the entire valley was reverberating, alive with the sounds emanating from a passionate battle for dominance.

As the rays of the early morning sun illuminated their intertwined naked bodies, Patty opened her eyes. She could still smell the masculine cologne in the air as she snuggled into Jay's chiselled body. She beamed with self-confidence, a big smile across her face, glad that she could still seduce men much younger than her. She lit a cigarette, her mind wandering over the happenings of the previous night. She was surprised by Jay's well-toned athletic body and unconventional moves. She liked him; he was direct, much like her, aggressive, a go-getter who knew what he wanted and would do all it took to achieve it.

She spoke aloud, blowing smoke on his face. 'So, Jay, what

is it that you want from me? While I would be delighted to live in the dream that it was my sexual appeal that drove you 2000 kilometres to Mashobra, you don't appear to be a man who lacks female attention. In fact, quite to the contrary, your moves were well-timed and very well-rehearsed. I appreciate experience when I see it, Jay.'

'Thank you, Patty; but you should have a little more confidence in yourself. I was drawn first to your delectable body and then to your comprehensive knowledge of the art industry. As I had mentioned to you previously, I am looking for an opportunity to deploy my money. However, unlike in the past when this would have meant making a passive investment in stocks, bonds and real estate, I wish to deploy it in a business opportunity where I can play a more active role. Based partly on my last discussion with you and partly on some research that I have done since then, I feel the art market in India presents such an opportunity. I was wondering if we could work together on a business plan. You could be the expert and I could bring the capital necessary to support our business.'

Patty evaluated Jay's offer. His strong muscular hands, tight buttocks and six-pack abs kept arising in her mind, clouding her thoughts. Could he be of any use? she wondered. Young men and money had been useful to her in the past. In any case, Jay couldn't do her any harm, it was worth exploring.

After a minute of silence, she finally spoke, driven by what she hoped was not just her lust and desire for him. 'If we wish to do business together, it is important that we build trust in each other. Based on my experience, I believe that professional relationships are successful only when there is a strong affinity and bond between the two parties. Why don't you move in with me? It will give us an opportunity to get to know each other better and I could then introduce you to the intricacies of the art business.'

Jay was a little foxed by Patty's proposal. While he had enjoyed the previous night, to move in with someone he barely knew made him uncomfortable. He enjoyed his personal space and didn't like people intruding on it. He was worried that before he had the opportunity to learn anything from Patty, he would end up having a disagreement with her on some frivolous matter and spoil his chances. Or even worse, like all the other women in his life, he would get bored of her.

However, despite his reservations, by the time they checked out of the hotel, Jay had decided to shift bag and baggage to Patty's house.

≈

Chapter 12

From Alpha Male to Eye Candy

Patty lived in a lavish farmhouse on the outskirts of Delhi, surrounded by nature. When Jay arrived, he was impressed by the manicured lawns that lay on either side of the driveway. The environment was quiet and serene, a huge contrast to the hustle bustle of Delhi. The house itself was immaculate; the interiors were tastefully done up, the working staff well trained and courteous, dressed all in white. Everything reflected the taste of its owner.

He was enamoured by the ambience. Despite his riches, he hadn't been able to enjoy greenery and empty space in Mumbai. He felt as if he were staying in a spa. The staff was not surprised to see him, a young man moving into the house. On the contrary, they showed a degree of finesse and familiarity which Jay presumed came from the experience of having served many like him before. Many had come before him and many more were likely to follow in the future.

He met Patty in the evening, once she came home from

the gallery. They gave each other a hug followed by a customary kiss on the cheek. After exchanging pleasantries, she asked him to join her in the bar in half an hour so that they could have a few drinks before heading to dinner. A little later, they were sipping martinis.

'So Patty, how do we proceed? What's the plan for tomorrow?'

'Tomorrow? Have patience, my dear. You need to relax, acclimatise yourself, become comfortable with your new surroundings. I will give you a glimpse into the lives of social glitterati; introduce you to the key influencers and trendsetters. Then gradually we will unlock the mysteries of running an art gallery successfully. And, by the way, just so you know, I have asked the staff to move your personal belongings into my room. I hope you weren't expecting a separate room?'

Over the next month, Jay accompanied her to various events: the opening of new galleries, the launches of new artists and exhibitions. These events were followed by well-organized parties where the social elite mingled with the larger art fraternity. He hated these parties but attended them nevertheless, hoping to meet some important influencers and trendsetters in the art fraternity. However, when he analysed his personal notes at the end of the month, he was disappointed to see that he had failed to meet even a single person of any significance. Most of his interactions were with people who were pests and social climbers, with little standing in the art fraternity, happy to get their free alcohol, hoping that the social standing of people around them would somehow rub off on them.

If he thought that his luck was going to change soon, he was in for a shock. As if the happenings of the last month were not bad enough, what followed was downright humiliating. He had to tag along with Patty to girly parties where he was introduced to middle-aged women who literally undressed him with their eyes as if he were a gigolo. Seeing the ferocity of their stares, he wondered if they had some background information on him that he wasn't aware of. Was Patty gossiping about her carnal exploits with her girlfriends? Sometimes, even a man as confident and seasoned as him felt uncomfortable.

Patty, on the other hand, beamed with glory, proudly showcasing her latest trophy. She had certainly gained many points within the social glitterati thanks to her latest acquisition. For his part, he played along; however, his patience was waning.

It was only after the first two months that the interactions and meetings became more meaningful. But even now, she was very careful not to introduce him to her inner circle. She had no intention of allowing him any role in her existing art business which primarily revolved around contemporary artists.

Frankly, she had had no idea how she was going to utilise him and his wealth when she asked him to move in with her. All she knew was that he was affluent, young and great in bed. This combination had never let her down in the past. If it weren't for her conversation with her lieutenant, Biswas Mukherjee, she would have soon gotten bored of Jay's antics and thrown him out of her house. However, Biswas convinced her that his wealth could come in handy to restart a quest she had abandoned a few years earlier for lack of funds. Unknown to the art fraternity, she had secretly ventured into collecting the paintings of the Navaratnas, nine artists who were recognised as national treasures. By the time she realised that she had bitten off far more than she could chew, the misadventure had cost her significantly and had to be abandoned midway. Consequently, she was stuck with over 200 paintings of the old masters which lay in her warehouse. If she could somehow convince Jay to partner with her in this venture, then she could utilise his wealth to create a market for these works. If successful, this venture could bring in tens of millions of dollars, but it was far too risky for her to put in her own capital.

It was with this hidden agenda that, over the next few months, she allowed him to accompany her to visit her art galleries on a more regular basis. She wanted him to understand the business tactics involved in running a successful art gallery in India. She knew that she needed to win his trust before offering him the chance to partner with her on the Navaratnas. Once he was sold on the macro dynamics of the market and raring to go, she would, after what appeared to be caution and deliberation, allow him an insight into the greatest investment opportunity in the art market.

Every fortnight, Patty travelled to Mumbai for a week to take stock of her gallery at Kala Ghoda and meet her important clients, connoisseurs, art critics and other influencers. There were two types of clients that galleries preferred. The first type consisted of art connoisseurs and museums—the trend-setters. They were the key influencers in the art market, signalling to the larger art audience that the artist had been endorsed and recognised. The art fraternity closely followed their actions and purchases in order to decipher new trends and artists. Their endorsement could catapult an artist into a new sphere of prestige, thereby increasing the value of his or her work exponentially. Since art by nature is a non-standardised commodity, its value is subjective, dependent on individual tastes and incapable of efficient pricing. In order to overcome this void, the art industry had carefully developed an intricate signalling process whereby the approval of a handful of art connoisseurs, critics, galleries and museums determined what was valuable and what was not.

A majority of the art museums in India were under government control. Patty enjoyed exploiting and entertaining their curators in expensive restaurants over bottles of wine, where a seven-course meal cost more than their monthly salary. She would be adequately robed, wearing dresses with deep necklines that showcased her well-endowed body, holding their hands and indulging in flirtatious talk. By the time the conversation moved to discussing business, they were so far down her cleavage that they had no credible chance of putting up a defence.

When it came to art connoisseurs, she was very conservatively dressed and always accompanied by her curator and lieutenant, Biswas Mukherjee. At these meetings, Biswas would indulge in artistic masturbation with the connoisseurs, subtly impressing them with his deep knowledge about the art industry and the latest developments in the area of provenance search and authentication.

'Did you know, Mr Jindal, Tagore was so modest about his artistic talent that he once remarked to Jamini Roy that since he didn't enjoy any formal training in an art school, his paintings were perhaps not complete in the way they should have been. However, Jamini Roy disagreed and praised his paintings for their inner strength, their inherent rhythm and reflection of artistic beauty.'

Patty, on the other hand, massaged their egos by praising their tastes, their existing collection of paintings and their latest acquisitions. She seconded their opinions, gradually introducing a few paintings which would supposedly enrich their existing collections.

'Sir, that Husain you picked up at the auction last month, right under the nose of Mittal—that was a brilliant master stroke, he didn't have a clue what hit him! I met his dealer after the auction. Asked him how his boss was. "Don't ask," he replied. Heard the poor fellow got fired the next week.'

The second type of clients consisted of art collectors and investors who were regular customers of the gallery and played by its well-defined rules. That is, they understood that investing in art was something done for the long term and selling a masterpiece was a very discreet and private affair best managed by the gallery from which it had been purchased. Hence, auctions which were too loud and public could not be in their best interest.

Patty dealt directly with her customers, selling them paintings at perceived discounts to the market, thereby encouraging them to buy more. In case they desired to sell a particular work, she went out of her way to find them buyers, even if it meant that she had to buy the painting for herself. Since all sales were routed through the gallery, clients were never aware whether a purchase had been made by the gallery on its own account or on behalf of another client. This helped to maintain confidence in the market. Her regular customers were seldom sellers, assured that the market in which they were invested was liquid and exit was a mere formality, possible on a moment's notice.

As for artists, they never dealt with clients directly, preferring to act through galleries which marketed their work while also creating their brand and reputation in the market. Patty hand-held the artists in her guild, exploiting her circle of influence to gradually introduce them to various collectors, connoisseurs and critics. While these meetings appeared casual and were usually conducted over a glass of wine, they were actually rehearsed and conducted in a controlled environment. She was always available, cutting in to rescue her artists at the first sign of the slightest discomfort. She mentored the artists personally and her gallery allocated substantial resources towards building their brand and market. However, it took several years to build the brand of an artist and for his works to mature and evolve. During this interim period, it was essential to manage the perception of the value of their works in the market. The perception that an artist was overhyped or overpriced could easily end his career.

Her gallery enjoyed complete control over the works of the artists she promoted. By exercising control on the supply, she was able to manipulate the prices of the work with ease. Once the tastes of the clients had been aligned by using different forms of influence, the artist would produce hundreds of pieces within a short period of time, often compromising on quality. She would evaluate the demand-supply situation and every time she perceived that the market was hot and prices would support it, go on a rampage selling artwork of the artist through exhibitions and art fairs. However, at all points of time, she would maintain close contact with her clients, keeping track of the movement of the paintings to ensure they didn't come back into the secondary market circulation, thereby competing with her own inventory.

Control over the market was extremely important and she didn't like entertaining clients who were known to flip paintings in their possession at art auctions. Art auctions were despised by her and other galleries alike as the price of the paintings became public knowledge and there were no inherent controls on who could bid for the work. However, she along with other galleries had come up with a unique system to ensure that paintings of artists backed by them were sold at higher prices. Art auctions allowed for anonymous buyers and sellers. Galleries often bid for works of their own artists in case they feared they wouldn't sell or would do so for a lower price.

One of the worst things a gallery could do was to overprice the work of an artist at an auction. If the work did not sell at that price point, then the price could not be lowered. Any reduction in price would reflect desperation and create panic in the market. It would send the wrong signal: that the artist was overpriced and therefore, adversely impact the credibility of the gallery and the artist alike. This was the reason why prices of art seldom saw any meaningful correction; the only thing that happened during periods of slowdown was that there were no transactions. The art market was opaque in its operation with both the prices and buyers being decided by the galleries in secrecy.

Jay wondered how, despite conflicts of interest and cartelisation, the art industry remained unregulated. In any other industry, such blatant cartelisation and manipulation would have immediately attracted the ire of the competition commission or some other regulator to protect consumer interest. However, all was fair in the unregulated art industry.

Chapter 13

Navaratnas—The Virgin Opportunity

It was past dinner on a cold winter night in Delhi. After a few drinks followed by a wholesome dinner, Jay was relishing a glass of Cointreau while Patty sipped on her cognac. He lay on the couch, cuddled in her arms next to the fireplace where a bright blaze warmed the living room.

Six months had passed since their encounter in Mumbai. During this period, he had learnt a lot about the art industry and gained valuable insights into the working of the galleries. Patty had assisted him with meeting some key influencers in the art fraternity. She had also ensured that he was kept at a distance from her high-networth clientele and regular customers.

However, unknown to Patty, Jay had succeeded in making a few introductions of his own in the exclusive art collectors' guild, assisted by none other than Biswas Mukherjee, her trusted lieutenant. Within a few weeks of arriving at her residence, Jay had realised that Biswas was central to her operations, a key functionary in the successful running of the galleries. He had used every available opportunity to build a relationship with him, exploiting his taste in cigars to create a camaraderie with him. Every time Patty travelled on business, Jay would land up at his house to enjoy the best single malts and the finest Cohibas. Though himself a teetotaller, Biswas was a very gracious host. They would drink and smoke till dawn, discussing the happenings in the art market. Biswas was overzealous in his mastery of the art industry and would continuously rant about his expertise in art history and research. Jay would indulge him, sometimes out of interest and sometimes because he had to learn.

'Jay, do you know why Tagore started painting?'

'No, sir, I don't.'

'You see, his original writings and poems were all written in Bengali; they were so deep in their thought and meaning that very few people could fully comprehend them and consequently, they often lost their meaning in translation. Even literary greats like W.B. Yeats, who translated several of Tagore's works, confessed that he often wondered if he had done justice to them. Hence, Tagore was thrilled when he began to explore art. For the first time, he had found a medium which did not require language to express itself. Since expression in art was independent of language, it was not restricted by the same limitations as writing.

'This is also the reason why Tagore never described or named his paintings. He didn't want to influence and restrict a person's imagination with his own thought process. His paintings could have different meanings for different people, depending upon their own imaginations.'

Jay would deliberately stoke Biswas's inner desire to assume a larger role.

'Sir, for a person of your calibre, with your knowledge and intellect, the position of a mere curator seems inappropriate, almost insulting. Anything less than a full-fledged partnership is not appropriate. If I had a venture, I would be proud and obliged to take you on as a partner, an equal and not a mere employee.'

On hearing this, Biswas would completely lose his cool, abusing the art fraternity and its commercialisation before yelling ... 'I am not subservient to anyone!'

Jay's thoughts suddenly wandered back to the silence in the room, broken only by the burst of embers from the firewood. He realised that he had been stroking Patty's arm all this time when his mind had been elsewhere.

Patty meanwhile was deep in thought herself.

'I must approach the subject delicately, he shouldn't feel pushed otherwise he will become cautious. I need to highlight the opportunity while downplaying the risks. I have successfully created a false sense of intimacy by taking him along for a few "pre-arranged" meetings, introducing him to a few unimportant people and giving him a very broad flavour of the art market. He should feel that it's because of this personal relationship, the fact that we feel comfortable in each other's company that I am making this offer to him. Under no circumstance should he feel that I am in distress.'

He could sense that she was uneasy about something. Something or someone was bothering her. 'What is it, darling?

You look a little lost tonight. Is something bothering you?'

She sighed and turned to look at him without speaking a word. 'So, I have his attention now.'

'You have started reading my mind quite well, perhaps a little too well for my comfort. Anyway, I am going to let you in on a business secret tonight. Frankly, I don't know why I am doing this, perhaps it is the alcohol that is mellowing my defences or maybe I feel that I can trust you and the time has come for us to take our relationship to another level. Whatever the reason, what I tell you next represents a great business opportunity that could very well alter the course of the art market in India as we know it today.'

Suddenly the casual atmosphere in the room became serious. Jay was curious and anxious. He knew from experience that there were no free lunches in the commercial world. What secret was she planning to reveal? Why was she opening her doors to him like this? What did she want in return?

She gave him another glance, he was now sitting upright, waiting anxiously for the words to come out of her mouth. So she began...

'In the year 1972, the Indira Gandhi government passed legislation declaring nine artists as Navaratnas, that is, the jewels of India—Abindranath Tagore, Rabindranath Tagore, Gaganendranath Tagore, Jamini Roy, Amrita Shergil, Raja Ravi Varma, Nandalal Bose, Nicholas Roerich and Sailoz Mookherjea.'

She paused, took a sip of her cognac and continued.

'The legislation aimed to recognise these nine artists as National Treasures and provide the necessary protection to their artwork. Consequently, they came under the purview of the Antiquities and Art Treasures Act, which specified that from the date of the enactment of the law, the works of these artists, many of whom were also active in the Indian independence movement, were not to be taken out of the country. The Act put complete restriction on the export and foreign ownership of their works.'

'But, what about the paintings acquired prior to the enactment of this law?' asked Jay.

'Good question,' replied Patty. 'These remained outside the ambit of the law and could be displayed at galleries or put up for bidding at auctions abroad.'

'Okay.'

'Further, while there was no explicit restriction on the ownership, purchase and sale of these artworks by citizens of India, the law empowered the central government to forcibly acquire works deemed valuable from private collections for the preservation of the national heritage and public display.'

Jay nodded his head in utter shock, 'But, this must have decimated their market.'

'You are right on track, Jay,' she replied. 'What followed was complete mayhem. Large collections belonging to distinguished families, art connoisseurs and collectors were forcibly acquired by the government at predetermined values and handed over to museums and galleries for public display. Many families disputed these acquisitions, resulting in suits that went on for decades. Even those people whose collections were not acquired decided to relinquish them, often selling them discreetly at distress prices.'

'I don't understand. Patty. Why did people whose collections were not compulsorily acquired, sell them and that too, under distress.'

'Fear and paranoia. No one wanted the hassle of dealing with the government. Very few people understood the law and even fewer could interpret it. In the absence of credible information and knowledge, there was panic and rumour-mongering in the market.'

'I understand now. Please continue.'

'What used to be prized possessions became liabilities overnight and consequently, the Navaratnas as a class of work were discarded by the elite, the connoisseurs and collectors alike.'

'So, are all of them with the government now?'

'No, not all of them. Post these acquisitions by the government, around 3000 works were estimated to have remained in private hands in India.'

'Okay.'

'However, the legislation created an imbalance in the art market, forcibly shifting customer tastes and preferences. With the Navaratnas becoming untouchables overnight, the art collectors and connoisseurs shifted their attention towards works of contemporaries who were not covered by the draconian provisions of this law and, therefore, non-controversial. This gave a sudden fillip to the demand for works of popular contemporaries like Husain, Raza, Souza, Mehta and Gaitonde amongst others.'

'I see,' replied Jay.

'Consequently, when the art industry exploded in the late

1980s and early 90s, the artwork of Rabindranath Tagore, Jamini Roy or Nandalal Bose did not receive the kind of exposure that a Husain, Raza or Mehta did. As a result, the best works of the younger generation of artists began to command their price in tens of millions of rupees, while the works of the Navaratnas, the few that were traded or bid for, sold at a fraction of their actual value. By regulating the ownership and consequently, the demand for their works, the legislation had effectively destroyed the market for them.'

'No wonder I haven't heard any records being broken by paintings of Tagore,' he replied. 'But wait a minute, you also mentioned Amrita Shergil—if my memory serves me well, her paintings go for millions. Am I correct?'

'Yes, you are correct, Jay.' The only exception was Amrita Shergil, a large portion of whose oeuvre had been created in Europe, exposed to western art collectors and consequently, commanding prices running into tens of millions of rupees.

'Okay. Now that I have the background, tell me about the business opportunity.'

'Hold on, I am coming to that in a bit, Jay,' she replied. 'My mouth is dry with all the speaking. Can you get me another cognac?'

Jay finished his Cointreau in a single gulp and rushed to the bar to get a refill for both of them.

She smiled as soon as he left for the bar; things appeared to be in order so far, not only did she have his attention, he also looked extremely excited. However, the next part was the most crucial; she reminded herself not to rush in and to take her time.

As he handed her the glass of cognac, she took a long sip while he waited in anticipation for her to commence.

'Ah! That was required,' she said aloud.

She could see the changing expressions on his face. He was getting impatient. She needed to start soon otherwise he might lose interest.

'However, times have changed since then,' she said. 'There are many in the government fraternity who feel that the Antiquities and Art Treasures Act belonged to a bygone era and has little relevance in today's world. Rather than recognising the nine artists and celebrating their work, the draconian provisions of the Act decimated their market. The same is also true for antiquities in India, whose market had never taken off thanks to the provisions of this Act. It had actually encouraged an underground market and smuggling in India. There is talk in the corridors of power that the Act might be repealed.

'Even if this doesn't happen, the domestic art market has evolved since the 1970s and now has a much larger base of investors and collectors. There is bound to be some domestic demand for the work of the Navaratnas.'

'Hmmmm. But operationally, is this feasible?' he asked.

'Of course! It is feasible. In fact, I have already commenced work. You know Biswas?'

Of course he knew Biswas. He had smoked a cigar at his house the previous weekend. However, he decided to feign ignorance and gave her a blank look instead.

'Biswas Mukherjee, the curator at my gallery, you met him once before.'

'Yes, I remember now,' he replied. 'What about him?'

'He is an expert on the Navaratnas. We ran a pilot project and within a short period of time acquired almost 200 paintings. So, I don't have any doubt in my mind that the acquisition can be done.'

He nodded his head in agreement but wasn't convinced.

'Further, you have already seen my hold on the art fraternity. I have the key influencers in my pocket, the connoisseurs, the museums. It will not be difficult for me to create the domestic market for the Navaratnas.'

'Wow. So what do you need me for?'

'I need you to bankroll this operation,' she replied. 'We can be equal partners in this project. I will bring the experience, knowhow and network, whereas you will bring in the capital. Together, we will be unstoppable, a force to reckon with.'

Jay didn't say a word—he was mesmerised by the presentation. What a brilliant sales spiel, he thought to himself. There was a tsunami of thoughts running in his mind. On one hand, he had no doubt that this was a great opportunity; the Navaratnas were available for throwaway prices right now. However, on the other hand, this was a highly risky venture. Patty had tried hard to underplay the risks involved. The paintings were widely distributed in private hands across the country and it would be a task of gargantuan proportions to aggregate them and then to create a market for them. No gallery had ever successfully attempted an operation to control such a large and widely distributed market and with no authority over supply, there wouldn't be any power over the price. This problem was unique and didn't arise in the case of contemporary artists who were associated with specific art galleries, which controlled the supply of their works in the market and consequently managed their prices. However, if some gallery did succeed in managing the supply and the market of the Navaratnas, then it would make a financial killing. They had enough intrinsic value to support their prices going up at least a few times over the next decade.

The silence was deafening. He could hear her heartbeat as she waited in anticipation for his response. However, he didn't intend on obliging her just yet. He needed to run the numbers in his mind and scope the opportunity. He didn't want to be rushed in. As it was well past midnight, he suddenly got up and kissed her goodnight on the cheek and proceeded to bed. He knew that he had a long night ahead of him; she would certainly corner him the next morning to give a response to her offer.

Patty looked intently at him as he left, trying hard to decipher his thoughts. Had she succeeded in stoking his curiosity and risk-taking appetite sufficiently to ensure he embarked on this risky journey with her? Had he taken the bait? Otherwise, she would be stuck with an inventory of over 200 paintings. They were gathering dust in her warehouse with no apparent buyers. She had almost a million dollars invested in these for over half a decade now. Money which could have been better utilised for buying contemporaries.

Jay lay wide awake in bed analysing the business opportunity. After a few hours of brainstorming, he had all the questions answered to make an informed decision.

The next morning as Jay approached the breakfast table,

he found Patty engrossed in the morning paper, sipping on her cup of tea. He had no way of knowing this, but Patty had been waiting anxiously for over an hour, pretending to be reading the headlines of the bloody paper.

'Good morning, Patty,' he said aloud.

She slowly folded the paper in her hand to look at him.

'Good morning, Jay,' she said. 'I didn't see you coming. Did you sleep well last night?'

If Jay could see behind her make-up, he would have noticed the dark circles under her eyes.

'Interesting you asked. I haven't slept the whole damn night thinking about the business opportunity.'

'Oh Lord!' she said. 'So what did you think?'

She wanted to sound casual, but there was nervousness in her voice.

'Well, you see, I am a novice in the art industry.'

'Yes, exactly, that's why you need a partner like me; someone who knows the ups and downs, who's been there, done that.'

She was almost sporting a smile now. This discussion was proceeding in the right direction. But just then, it all changed.

'Yes, you are right. However, I believe that trying to create a market for a genre of artists whose market does not exist is fraught with too much risk and uncertainty. There is no doubt in my mind that if I agreed to pursue this path, then you would be the perfect partner. However, I am sorry. That is not my intention and hence I will have to respectfully decline your offer.'

He watched the growing disappointment on her face as

she continued to butter the toast in complete silence. He was extremely excited about the opportunity to acquire and manipulate the Navaratnas. However, he didn't wish to share the bounty with anyone else. If he was organising the capital, then he would have it all for himself. He felt confident that he could do it on his own. After all, he had been successful in every venture he had participated in till date. Patty had revealed her cards by introducing him to the key influencers in the market. She was of little use to him now. If at all, he would need the services of an art expert. Patty had mentioned that Biswas had played a critical role in the acquisition of the Navaratnas.

What followed came as a surprise to him. After all, till yesterday, they were talking about their growing relationship built on mutual trust and comfort.

She said abruptly, 'Then so be it, Mr Malhotra. We will have to cut short our little arrangement. Please pack your bags and leave the house. I do not wish to see you when I return from the gallery in the evening.'

He had obviously outlived his hospitality and utility for Patty.

≈

Chapter 14

Belling the Cat

Six weeks had elapsed since the fateful day when Patty had unceremoniously thrown him out of her house. Jay's self-esteem and ego had taken a beating, badly bruised by the treatment meted out to him. Nothing like this had ever happened to him. On the contrary, it was he who had behaved in a similar fashion on various occasions, throwing countless women out of his house, sometimes even forgetting their names in the morning. It certainly didn't feel good to be on the other side of the table.

However, true to his character, he had immediately bounced back, not wasting any time on gaining sympathies. Life had to move on, he had to chart the future course of action and constructively plan his next move while simultaneously reaching out to his high-networth clientele. There was no turning back; he was completely sold on the idea of the Navaratnas. In fact, he had found it difficult to hide his excitement and awe when he was listening to the story narrated by Patty, often checking himself from making stupid remarks that might highlight his excitement. Now all he needed to do was to convince his clients to make an investment in the business venture under his able captainship.

His high-networth clients were people who had amassed exorbitant wealth over the past decade, partly on his advice and consequently, had sworn allegiance to him. They were not very well informed about the nuances of the art market but were extremely sharp when it came to making money, wandering in the open oceans much like sharks evaluating opportunities to strike. However, when Jay ran them through his plan of acquiring and monopolising the market of the Navaratnas, even they were shocked. He explained to them that he needed each one of them to contribute $3 million to this cause and if he was successful, the sky was the limit. Armed with a war chest of $15 million, he proceeded to undertake the challenging task of discreetly acquiring artworks of the Navaratnas.

He knew that it was critical for him to acquire the paintings that lay in Patty's warehouse. She had mentioned around 200 of them. In the absence of a domestic market, these paintings must be catching dust. He could use the adverse circumstances to his benefit to strike a hard bargain with her, providing his new venture a huge push. However, this was easier said than done. She would suspect him the moment she received a query. He had to act carefully to make his venture successful.

When Biswas reached the gallery the next morning, he was informed by the staff that there was a prospective client waiting in his room, sipping tea. He had shown an interest in the Jamini Roy that hung on the opposite wall and had enquired if there were any more available at the gallery.

'Hello! I believe you are looking for some Jamini Roys,' Biswas said when he entered his office. 'I am Biswas Mukherjee, the curator of this gallery. How may I help you Mr...?'

'Uday Jayashankar,' the man said.

'It is a pleasure to meet you, Mr Jayashankar. What can I do for you?'

'I am interested in paintings by the old masters, the Navaratnas. Do you have any works done by Tagore, Nandalal Bose and Raja Ravi Varma in addition to Jamini Roy?'

'Oh yes! We do. I am a little curious about your interest in the old masters. People usually come here looking for works by contemporary painters.'

'Mr Mukherjee, I represent a family from south India. They are very keen to acquire works by the old masters to add to their existing collection. The payment will be made on the spot after examining the paintings for their condition and provenance.'

'Perhaps I know of this family?'

'You might. However, on this occasion, they wish to remain anonymous. I hope this is not a problem?'

'No problem at all! Let me showcase the few paintings that are currently in the gallery. Then, depending on your appetite, we can pull out some more from the warehouse.'

Much to Biswas' surprise, within the next half hour, Mr Jayashankar had made an offer for the six paintings that lay in the gallery. The offer was much below their listed price, but it was an offer nonetheless.

Biswas had never seen anything like this before and was bewildered. He called up Patty, informing her of the mysterious customer and his offer on the paintings.

'He is asking for a bulk discount.'

'Bulk discount? Are you serious? Is he buying potatoes in the local mandi? Who the fuck does he think he is? Have you heard of him?'

'No, I haven't. Claims to represent some family in the south. In thirty minutes flat he made me an offer for six paintings.'

'Thirty minutes? That's insane. How does he wish to pay?'

'On the spot, in cash.'

'New money, is it?'

'Can't say. Maybe.'

'Huh, nothing surprises me anymore. Anyway, please proceed. But tell him that you are making an exception for him. I don't want word getting out that we are giving bulk discounts at our gallery. Also, don't disclose any information about the inventory of paintings in the warehouse. I want to meet this Jayashankar fellow before we proceed any further. I will catch an evening flight back to Delhi and be at the gallery in the morning. Ask him to come then and take his contact details if you can.'

Biswas congratulated Mr Jayashankar on his purchase and requested him to visit the gallery the next day for a meeting with Patty. He promised that in the interim, he would request the staff to retrieve a few paintings from the warehouse and make them available for display the next day. However, before he could ask him any further questions, including his contact details, Jayashankar was gone.

Patty called up a few galleries in Mumbai to find out the identity of this investor. Had any of them been approached by an intermediary representing a family from the south? She didn't get any affirmative answers. She was intrigued. Who had suddenly taken an interest in the Navaratnas?

It was only after she had boarded the flight that the thought suddenly dawned on her that this person could be a front for Jay Malhotra. She was amused at the thought. Poor Jay, did he really think that he could create a market for the Navaratnas? Hah, no way.

No sooner had she landed in Delhi than she called up Biswas. It was way past eleven at night and he was fast asleep. He looked at the phone, annoyed, mulling over whether to take the call or not.

'This better be important, Patty, I was sleeping.'

'It's Jay Malhotra!'

'What?'

'The mystery client is a front for Jay Malhotra. I am sure it is him.' Patty's excitement woke Biswas up.

'How does it matter if it is Jay Malhotra?'

'It doesn't. Frankly, I don't care who it is. These paintings are dead wood. Much of my money is stuck in them and I would be pleased to get rid of them.'

'Exactly, that's my view too. He is coming to the gallery tomorrow at eleven. You can see him then. Goodnight for now.'

But Biswas lay awake for some time, wondering why Jay

had not informed him of his plans. Did he not trust him?

Patty arrived at the office at half past ten the next morning. She was very excited about her meeting with Uday Jayashankar. She had little doubt in her mind that he was a mere front for Jay. She had lost her cool with Jay after he had declined her offer of a business partnership and on the spur of the moment, she had thrown him out of her house only to regret her decision later that night when she lay alone in bed.

Did Jay think that she was fool enough not to see through this farce? Or maybe he had taken her actions very personally and didn't wish to confront her. Oh dear! She almost felt sorry for him. Given a chance, she might forgive him and take him back. Her nights had become long and dull; she could do with some excitement and action.

Her excitement was short-lived. Uday Jayashankar was nothing like Jay Malhotra. He was uncouth, a big bore, a shrewd bastard who tirelessly negotiated every last penny. He drove such a hard bargain with Patty that at one point she had almost decided she could not and should not deal with him. After a few weeks of intense negotiation involving several rounds of give and take, a deal was finally struck between them whereby Patty agreed to sell the paintings in her possession for \$1.2 million. This was far short of the amount that she had hoped to get prior to the start of the negotiations. While disappointed with the results, she knew she had no choice. The paintings were no good for her, blocking capital which could be put to better use.

When Uday Jayashankar left her gallery after negotiating the purchase of the final tranche, she couldn't help but tell him that she would have much rather dealt with Jay himself than one of his cronies. The expression on Uday's face told her what she had known all along.

Later that evening, Uday Jayashankar met with his benefactor Jay Malhotra for a drink and narrated the incident to him.

'Jay, she knew that I was acting on your behalf.'

'I suspected that. In fact, I depended on it to make this plan successful.'

'What do you mean?' asked Uday.

'I had to exploit her ego, give her the false impression that I was digging my own grave, otherwise she wouldn't have ever sold us the paintings,' replied Jay. 'I knew that she would be able to see through the façade. However, I also knew that her personal ego and overconfidence would ensure that she downplayed our chances of success and sold us the paintings. After all, how could an art outsider succeed on a project that the queen of the market had failed herself?'

'Oh! I see.'

'Now that we have the paintings in our hand, the time has come for me to pull the rug from under her feet,' said Jay smilingly.

'What do you mean, pull the rug from under her feet?' asked Uday.

'Poach Biswas Mukherjee, her trusted lieutenant,' replied Jay.

'You mean the curator?' asked Uday. 'Why did you wait so long? It would have made my job so much easier.'

'No, it wouldn't have,' replied Jay. 'On the contrary, Patty wouldn't have sold us a single painting had she known that Biswas was on our side. We have the paintings in our possession only because of her strong belief that as outsiders, we will fail miserably in our venture to acquire and manipulate the market of the Navaratnas. However, the odds significantly change in our favour the moment Biswas comes on board.'

'How are you so sure that he will jump the ship?'

'Trust me, I know him well. He will. I have read him very closely.'

In his heart Jay hoped that Biswas would join him. If he didn't then this venture would be in peril. During the past six weeks, he tried desperately to connect with his network in the art fraternity, the insiders and influencers he had met on several occasions with Patty. These were the contacts he hoped to exploit to make his venture successful. He had built a rapport with these people, shared drinks with them and also the occasional joke. He was confident that they would reciprocate his niceties. However, his attempts to establish contact had been largely futile. He soon realised to his discomfort that people who did extend him courtesies were not important and the ones who were actually important didn't think much of him beyond a boy toy who had been discarded by his previous owner.

Exactly a month after the purchase of the last tranche was concluded, Biswas Mukherjee resigned from his curatorial responsibilities to join Jay Malhotra on the adventure of a lifetime and a truly momentous role, which he hoped would allow him to bring the Navaratnas back from oblivion.

Patty, who had been sporting a smile all this time, even

contemplating the possibility of enjoying the warmth of Jay's body, finally understood the true extent of his plan. The smile on her face died. She had been out-manoeuvred, taken for a ride. Her ego and self-esteem were hurt. What had appeared to her to be a good business decision only a month ago had suddenly turned sour. She was in a rage and longed to take revenge when the time was right.

Chapter 15

Line, Colour and Brush Strokes

Jay was happy. He had thoroughly enjoyed pulling the rug from under Patty's feet. He felt good and was in high spirits knowing that Patty must be furious with him. This was just payback. She shouldn't have thrown him out of the house.

His quest to acquire the Navaratnas had started on a good note. He now owned almost 200 paintings for a little over a million dollars. More importantly, he had Biswas Mukherjee, an art historian and expert, on his side. Biswas was the key to open the doors to the old world, giving him access to collectors, connoisseurs and old families from the nooks and corner of the country.

He had worked diligently on Biswas, analysing him closely, understanding his personality, his goals and ambition, his likes and dislikes. Biswas had a complex personality to say the least. However, once you understood his goals and ambition, it was easy to manipulate him.

Biswas had accepted the curatorial responsibility at Patty's gallery because he had found the environment at Shantiniketan slow and frustrating, almost suffocating. They were out of sync with the current times; he needed a platform which was flexible, without restrictions and most of all, he required higher budgetary allocations to pursue his scholarly activities. Besides, Patty had also agreed to sponsor the Catalogue Raisonné on Tagore. So far so good, but once the catalogue was finished in 1995, Biswas had found himself spending his time pursuing operational and commercial responsibilities which came along with the curatorial job. He despised selling works to clients and organising exhibitions to meet the costs of the gallery. He felt humiliated when Patty showed him off to her most coveted clients as a prized possession, commercially exploiting his artistic knowledge and research. He couldn't come to terms with the fact that despite his far superior knowledge and understanding of art history and research, Patty didn't treat him as an equal, often ordering him around.

Jay had noticed Biswas's simmering discontent and successfully exploited it to convince him to break his association with Patty and join him in his quest to aggregate and create a domestic market for the Navaratnas. He knew that money meant very little to Biswas, so he reached out to the art lover in him.

'Let us join hands as partners in this quest. Its ramifications are so great that it will alter the course of the art market, re-establishing the Navaratnas to their erstwhile position of glory as the jewels of India.'

There was no way Biswas could have refused such an offer. How could he hold back from such a noble cause?

Jay met him for dinner the next day to chart out their future course of action.

'Jay, acquiring the paintings from Patty was a master stroke. I had no idea that you were behind it. Why didn't you tell me in advance? I was wondering if I had lost my friend.'

'Biswas, you are good man, you have a conscience, a word which has little meaning for business people like me. I kept you in the dark as there was a conflict of interest. I knew that you wouldn't feel comfortable involving yourself in the sale of paintings while knowing that you would be leaving the gallery soon.

'Further, I also feared that Patty might see through your discomfort, thereby jeopardising our entire plan. In fact, I feel that your ignorance might have actually helped to calm her nerves, facilitating the sale of paintings to us.'

Biswas mulled over Jay's reply and then spoke after a moment's pause.

'Oh! Yes, you are quite right. I would have definitely been outside my comfort zone. By the way, I expect the next leg of your quest to be much more complicated. Buying paintings from collectors and connoisseurs is a different ball game altogether.'

'Why?' asked Jay.

'You see, art galleries look at paintings as trading stock. There is no emotional attachment. Every piece of art in a gallery is for sale at the right price. However, the same is not true for collectors and connoisseurs. They are generally very attached to the paintings in their possession. Some feel a sense of remorse, conflict and even guilt when asked to sell a painting in their possession.

'A few generations earlier, selling art was generally associated with the three D's: Debt, Death and Divorce. It had such a negative connotation that very few people actually came out in the open to acknowledge that they needed help.

'Then there are those collectors who are hesitant to sell their paintings before they have fully realised their value, so much so that most of the artwork never makes it to the market.'

'I see,' said Jay. 'So what is the way forward? How should I go about doing this?'

'Well, you will have to understand their psyche before approaching them. There are sensitivities involved. The discussion regarding sale has to be approached very delicately; otherwise, you risk the possibility of offending them. In which case, you would have overstayed your hospitality and the entire effort would be a non-starter. Then there is another problem.'

'What is that?'

'If word gets out about your quest, stating that a person or gallery is accumulating paintings of the old masters, then not only will the prices rise exponentially but a large number of prospective sellers will wait on the sidelines, hoping for still higher prices, thereby drastically reducing the availability of paintings in the market. For this quest to be successful, it is essential that we are discreet and maintain the highest level of confidentiality.

'And one last thing before we leave: you need to brush up on your knowledge of appreciating and understanding art and provenance research. The people you will be interacting with are no longer the party-goers at the cocktail circuit. You will meet with collectors and connoisseurs who know their art, who know the paintings in their possession like the back of their hands. You need to be well read, otherwise they will not respect you. You need to share your passion for art with them. Only then will your meetings be successful. Only then will you be able to enter into a deep conversation with them, convincing them to part with their family treasures.

'Go home and sleep well tonight, Mr Malhotra. Your education begins tomorrow.

'Also, bring two paintings along with you when you come tomorrow, one belonging to Raja Ravi Varma and the other of Tagore. I want our sessions to be practical.'

Jay reached Biswas' house early in the morning. Biswas was waiting for him dressed in his crisp kurta-pyjama.

'Show me the paintings that you have brought,' Biswas said.

As Jay handed him the paintings, Biswas's eyes lit up, 'Oh! Lovely,' he said excitedly. 'Raja Ravi Varma and Tagore represent two extremes of the curve. One was classically trained whereas the other didn't have any formal training and was an expressionist. These differences will become distinct to you as we progress during the course of the day.

'So what do you know about art appreciation?'

'Not much. Actually, nothing.'

'Nothing! Well I am not surprised. I have met a lot of people in the art fraternity—most of them don't know anything.'

'And what about the remainder?'

'They are liars.'

'That can't be true, Biswas. I mean, I have often heard people discussing lines, brush movements and colours on the cocktail circuit. They must know something.'

'Oh! Of course, these are much abused words. I once spoke to a gentleman over a glass of wine about the strength of lines in an impressionist work. Do you understand why that's funny?'

'Yes, I think I do. Wasn't impressionism about capturing the moment, that is, portraying the overall visual effects rather than details?'

'Yes, exactly, and hence colours took precedence over lines and contours. In order to appreciate a painting, you need to understand both the background of the artwork as well as evaluate the artwork itself. Lines, brush movement and colours deal with the latter. Let's start with these first and then we can move to the background later.

'The skill of an artist is reflected in the strength and confidence of his lines. The line was regarded by the Renaissance experts as the most fundamental attribute in the structure of a painting. In fact, when the Great European School of Fine Arts opened, it aimed at teaching pupils how to draw rather than paint.'

'But, Biswas, I have seen a lot of artists drawing straight lines. Is that really such a big deal? How do you differentiate the boys from the men?'

'If an artist can draw a perfect circle with a single continuous stroke of his brush then you know that you are looking at someone who has exceptional control over his lines,' explained Biswas.

'Oh! So this is a litmus test for differentiating the boys from the men? Interesting.'

'Look at the strength and confidence of the lines in the Raja Ravi Varma. In contrast, Tagore was an expressionist and hence the emphasis in his works was not on lines and forms as can be seen from the wild brush movements in this painting.'

'Ah! I see,' replied Jay. 'The difference in their styles is so stark.'

'This brings us to the next important aspect, the brushwork.

'Brushwork can be slow, precise and controlled, or rapid, casual and loose. The nature of brushwork is determined by the style of the artwork rather than the temperament of the artist. Generally, you will find that the brushstrokes of realist painters are more precise and controlled than that of expressionists. Look at the controlled brushwork in the Raja Ravi Varma in contrast to the wild brush movements in the Tagore.

'When impressionists held their first exhibition in the nineteenth century, the public and critics were shocked by the loose and wild brush movements. In order to truly appreciate and decipher the image, they had to stand a few feet away from the artwork, quite the opposite of what they were used to.'

'I can only imagine,' replied Jay. 'It must have created quite a stir. And what about colour?'

'Hold on to your horses. We are getting there.

'As you probably know, colour has a major influence on our emotions and therefore, plays an important role in art. Generally speaking, bright colours stimulate positive emotional responses like happiness and exuberance whereas dark colours connote a sense of murkiness and sadness. Historically, impressionism and expressionism were the first movements to truly exploit the full potential of colour.

'Academic painters like Raja Ravi Varma adhered to conventional colour schemes—green grass, blue or grey sky—but it was modern artists who painted what they saw (impressionism) or how they felt (expressionism). A good example is the red sky in *The Scream* by Edvard Munch. Look at how the artist has captured the emotion and lent character to the figure. Similarly, several paintings by Mark Rothko consist of vast abstract canvasses soaked with bright colours such as yellow, orange, red, blue and indigo to stimulate an emotional response from the spectator.

'Let's now evaluate the Tagore. Look how he has used contrasting colours in this painting to seek an emotional response from his audience. Do you notice something peculiar? There is no usage of red and green in the painting.'

'But why?' asked Jay.

'Because Tagore was colour blind,' smiled Biswas.

Jay smiled, 'An expressionist who was colour blind, interesting.'

'Let's discuss content and composition now.

'Content and subject matter help us in understanding the message behind the painting. What does the artist wish to say? Who are the characters in the painting and what do they imply? Is the painting showcasing a historical or religious event? Generally, a still life is symbolic in nature and the different objects displayed have some symbolic representation.

'Composition, on the other hand, is important because it impacts the visual layout of the painting. A well composed painting will guide the eyes of the spectator to specific parts that the artist wishes him or her to see and highlight. Generally, artists who excel at composition are classically trained.

'Now, look at the Raja Ravi Varma. What is the first thing that you see when you look at the painting?'

'The eyes of the woman,' replied Jay.

'Exactly. This is a fine example of composition. The artist wanted you to see the eyes of the woman. He perhaps wanted you to appreciate the surroundings from her perspective.'

'Oh! I see,' replied Jay. 'I never thought about this.'

'So are you with me so far? Can we now commence our discussion regarding the background and context of the artwork?'

'I guess so. I mean, I have heard you, Biswas. I still need to read more on the subject matter to grasp it better. Even then, I don't think I will ever develop the understanding that you have on the subject.'

'Obviously, you will not, Jay. The objective is to ensure that you can stand your ground. I have an idea. Once we finish these discussions, you and I can spend the next few days evaluating some of the other paintings in your possession.'

'That's a great idea, Biswas. I will pull out a dozen paintings and bring them along with me.'

'Make sure you get a mixed bag, a few Jamini Roys, some Tagores, Raja Ravi Varma and so on. They all have different styles and I will highlight the differences. It will facilitate your understanding of the subject.

'Okay. Now let's return to our discussion.

'The background and context can answer questions relating

to when and where a painting is created, its affiliation to a school or movement, its style, whether it is abstract or representational, at what stage of development the artist was at in his career when it was created and so on.

'The date can tell you about the methodology adopted or the material/medium used in the creation of the painting. Artworks which belong to a specific school or movement have similar styles of workmanship that can provide insights into their composition and meaning. For example, in Egyptian art, the size of the figures reflected their social status and only six colours were used, each having their own significance. Dutch realist artists appreciated exact, life-like replication of interiors and surroundings, except in portraiture, where the intention was to flatter the subject. Cubists rejected the normal rules of linear perspective and, instead, disassembled their subject into a series of flat transparent geometric plates that overlapped and intersected at different angles.

'Artwork comes in different forms like landscape, portraiture, genre-paintings (everyday scenes), history and still life. In historical Europe, these genres were ranked on the basis of the clarity with which they could disseminate and communicate moral messages. Religious art often had to comply with specific rules regarding composition, subject and theme. This was especially true for Christian themes which were depicted in Renaissance art. While depicting Jesus Christ as a child, the artist always used the facial expressions of a fully grown adult, expressing the divine status of the subject.

'Knowing where and under what circumstances an artwork was created often allows us to better understand and appreciate the work at hand. Monet devoted his life to painting in the outdoors and had a Japanese water garden created next to his house. It was here that he painted a series on water lilies in the later part of his life. Pissarro mostly painted outdoors, always under pressure to finish his work before the fading sunlight. This found reflection in his brushwork, which was fast and loose. Michelangelo painted the ceiling of the Sistine Chapel over a four-year period by balancing himself on a scaffolding.

'The surroundings can also have a major impact on the mood of the artist and therefore, find reflection in his work. Van Gogh created paintings in the 1880s exhibiting dark colours, perhaps reflecting the period of acute poverty in the Netherlands. However, this completely changed when he later moved to Paris and was influenced by impressionism; his paintings now exhibited bright colours.

'Now let's re-evaluate this Tagore. It is a landscape. Tagore was known to paint landscapes in a single sitting, standing outside his house in the open, surrounded by the lush environs of Shantiniketan. He did this either early in the morning to capture the impact of the light from the rising sun on the surroundings, or late in the evening when the sun was setting and the light was fading.

'Given the fast and loose brush movements in this particular painting, if I were to make an informed guess, I would say that it was created in the late evening under the pressure of the fading light.

'Artists typically evolve in their style of work, improving their techniques with the passage of time, achieving a zenith and declining into a nadir in their later years. Understanding the background of the artist can help us identify the influences in his life which found reflection in his artwork. The Norwegian expressionist Edvard Munch never completely recovered from some early deaths in his family. His consequent disturbed nature could be seen in many of his works. The same is also true for Rabindranath Tagore who was also influenced by the deaths in his family.

'With that, we end our discussions, Jay. I hope you enjoyed listening as much as I enjoyed narrating the history of art.'

'I thoroughly enjoyed the session, Biswas. I have learnt more today than in all the time I spent with Patty. In fact, it makes me wonder, did you ever spend the same amount of time with Patty on this subject?'

'I tried, Jay, I really tried. But over a period of time, I realized that she wasn't really interested in art—it was money she was after.'

'Hmmm...interesting, Biswas. Anyway, I will organise the paintings and bring them along with me when we meet next. I am very excited about testing my theoretical knowledge practically.'

'Let's do that over the coming week. We can thereafter spend some time understanding provenance and art authentication.'

≈

Chapter 16

Provenance is Money

Jay was raring to go and was getting increasingly impatient at the slow pace of progress. They had spent the last few weeks discussing art appreciation by evaluating several paintings in his possession. What had started out as an interesting exercise, had soon become mundane and repetitive.

'Jay, now that you are well versed in art appreciation, we should spend some time understanding art provenance and authentication,' said Biswas.

'Is it necessary to learn about provenance? It sounds very theoretical and boring. Is it relevant to the quest?' asked Jay.

Biswas didn't take very kindly to his words and there was an immediate reprisal, which left Jay foxed.

'You think I am an idiot wasting my time on something that is not relevant?' shouted Biswas. 'I don't care if you find it boring. It is very relevant, as it decides the value of a painting. In any case, I will be only familiarising you with the subject. I don't expect you to master something that scholars spend their entire lives studying. A brief understanding of provenance will ensure that you ask the right questions of the owners of the paintings.'

'Oh! I see,' said Jay. 'I was only asking.'

'The answer to these questions will provide clues on whether further work is required to prove the provenance of the painting or not. Similarly, there are always tell-tale signs on the frame of the painting or on the canvas which can be deciphered by a person looking out for them.'

'Okay. So let's begin, Biswas.'

'Provenance refers to the chronology of the ownership, custody or location of a historical object. The primary purpose of tracing provenance is to provide contextual and circumstantial evidence for its original production or discovery by establishing, as far as possible, its history, especially the sequence of its formal ownership, custody and place of storage.'

'Biswas, are you suggesting that if records of a particular event don't exist, I mean, if there is no documentary evidence to corroborate an event, then in the art world it would not exist nor would it be recognised?'

'Exactly, Jay. You hit the nail on the head. Theoretically, the objective of provenance research is to produce a complete list of owners (together, where possible, with the supporting documentary proof) from when the painting was commissioned or in the artist's studio through to the present time. In practice however, there are usually gaps in the list and documents go missing or are lost.

'During my scholarly days in Shantiniketan, I came across almost a dozen paintings which despite their incomplete provenance appeared to have been created by the Grand Master, Rabindranath Tagore. I presented my findings to the evaluation board at Shantiniketan, and after a few months of critical analysis, almost all of them were attributed to the Grand Master as new findings.'

'So, how do you go about researching provenance, Biswas?'

'Well, there are several ways, Jay. The painting may have been part of an exhibition, or discussed or illustrated in print. If it has been in private hands on display in a stately home, it may be recorded in an inventory. It may have been noticed by a visitor who subsequently wrote about it, or mentioned it in a will or a diary. Where the painting has been bought from a dealer or changed hands in a private transaction, there may be a bill of sale or sales receipt that provides evidence of provenance. Auction records are also an important resource that assist in the research of provenance of paintings.

'If an artist is well known, a Catalogue Raisonné may exist listing his entire known works and their location at the time of writing. That reminds me, Jay; please carry a copy of the Catalogue Raisonné I had authored on Rabindranath Tagore with you. It will help you in your quest.

'Photographic evidence is also an important source of information. Historic photos may exist discussing and illustrating the works of the artist, period or genre. Similarly, a photograph of a painting may show inscriptions (or a signature) that was subsequently lost as a result of overzealous restoration. Conversely, a photograph may show that an inscription was not visible at an earlier date.'

'Why has provenance become so important in today's art

world, Biswas? What has changed? I guess it should have always been relevant.'

'Today, it is more relevant than ever before. Forgeries are widespread and legal battles over the authentication of paintings are shaking the foundation of the art market. Given this background, tracking provenance has increasingly gained importance. Further, provenance can have a huge effect on the value of the painting. If an art piece can boast an impressive provenance, having been part of a renowned collection or exhibited in an important institution or museum, this will affect its cultural value.

'At a Sotheby auction, an untitled Mark Rothko (*Yellow, Pink, Lavender on Rose*) belonging to the private collection of David and Peggy Rockefeller was showcased. The painting had hung on David Rockefeller's office wall for half a century. Since the proceeds from the auction of this painting were meant to go to charity, David Rockefeller allowed himself to be photographed with the painting. Sotheby carried out an aggressive marketing campaign leaning heavily on the Rockefeller provenance. The painting sold for $72.8 million. The next day at an auction held by Christie's, another Rothko from the same series of a similar size and date was sold for $29.9 million. You can argue that the exceptional provenance was responsible for the substantial price difference between the two artworks.

'Conversely, an incomplete provenance can raise serious legal issues, reducing the chances of selling a painting. Therefore, a well-documented provenance is fundamental for legal and commercial purposes. Any buyer would aim to minimise the chances of buying a stolen work and a work of art is more likely to be sold if its ownership is indisputable.'

'But you mentioned earlier that in real life, provenance is often incomplete. Then how do you go about authenticating paintings in these cases?'

'The authentication process can become difficult and time-consuming when the provenance is questionable. This might happen because of the loss of records, a simple lack of thorough documentation or natural disasters such as fire or flood. For example, from 1933 to the end of the Second World War in 1945, almost 20 per cent of all European art was plundered or destroyed by the Nazi regime. It began with Hitler denouncing all modern art as degenerate, including Cubism, Futurism and Dadaism, all of which he considered the product of a decadent twentieth-century society. All modern art found in German museums was sold or destroyed. Later, art and other antiques were plundered from the occupied territories for the Führermuseum. Art collections from prominent Jewish families including the Rothschilds, Rosenbergs, Wildensteins and Schlosses were confiscated. Also, Jewish art dealers often sold their collections to German galleries under distress. By the end of the war, hundreds of thousands of cultural objects had been amassed. In such circumstances, when supporting historical information is not available, scientific and stylistic analyses become critical in establishing authenticity.

'The first step in scientific analysis is an accurate characterisation of materials such as pigments, media, supports and binders. Once the components of an artwork have been identified, the results so obtained can thereafter be compared to other known works by the artist from the same period to check for consistency. Similarly, microscopic examination of paint cross-sections can reveal clues to the technique used by the artist which is information that aids stylistic evaluation of a work of art. Chemical analysis reveals identity and composition of historic and modern pigments and dyes. Medium analysis (oil, waxes, tempera, proteins, gums, synthetics) also reveals the artist's technique and identification of synthetic materials can provide an estimated date of creation. Together, historical research, scientific analysis and stylistic analysis can be a powerful tool to unravel the mystery of a painting.'

'So is this is a foolproof system of authentication, Biswas?'

'How can it be foolproof? This system of authentication is subjective; it is at best an opinion, based on various parametres and evidence, each of which can be assigned different importance to arrive at differing results. This system can at best be used to check a painting for inconsistencies, which if found, would indicate the likelihood of a forgery.

'As the price of paintings of masters increases to tens and hundreds of millions of dollars, so does the quality of forgeries entering the marketplace. This constant battle between new evolving methods of art authentication and high-quality forgeries is likely to continue in the future. The dynamics of the art forgery industry are so lucrative that even if one painting out of a hundred passes the existing art authentication methodologies, there is sufficient profit on the table and encouragement for the forgery industry to flourish.'

≈

Chapter 17

The Hunt for the Navaratnas

'Jay, I think you are ready to begin your quest.'

'You mean I know enough? I have been waiting to hear these words for a while but after the last episode, didn't want to offend you.'

'Jay, that was a spur-of-the-moment emotional outburst. I didn't mean to get you worried. I just wanted you to be well prepared.

'Anyway, let's not fool ourselves. You are no expert, but you possess sufficient knowledge to stand your ground. There is no end to what I can teach you but the effort to reward ratio is no longer favourable.'

'I am excited, Biswas. Raring to go. Where do we start?'

Biswas could see the rising impatience in Jay's body language.

'We should split our plan into two legs, each requiring the same amount of time and effort. The first leg will focus on West Bengal. This is where it all started—I mean the Bengal

School. The Tagores, Jamini Roy, Nandalal Bose, they all come from here. I expect the maximum reward for our effort in the first leg, both in terms of availability of paintings and their prices. We will concentrate our work in Kolkata, Howrah, Asansol, Durgapur and Siliguri. I am very well networked in Bengal and will be able to provide you inroads and meetings with collectors and connoisseurs, families of artists and old galleries.

'In the second leg, we will focus our attention on the erstwhile princely estates in British India like Travancore, Mysore, Hyderabad, Baroda, Gwalior, Udaipur, Jaipur and Varanasi. These were at the forefront of the promotion of art and culture in the nineteenth and early twentieth centuries. While they didn't actively promote the Bengal School, by virtue of being important centres for art and culture, I suspect a lot of paintings may have found their way into these cities.'

'This is very interesting, Biswas. However, I am a little curious that you didn't mention the cities of Delhi and Mumbai.'

'I have my reasons, Jay. Patty focused on those two while aggregating the Navaratnas which are now in your possession. She didn't want to dirty her shoes walking in the muck of the old world and hence chose the easier path of raiding the galleries in the two cities. Hence, I don't think you will find much success. The low hanging fruits have already been plucked and those that remain are high up in the tree and difficult to reach. Further, the art community is very closely knit in these cities. Your actions will be noticed and word will get out that you are aggregating the Navaratnas, making their availability more difficult and costly. We will hit Mumbai and Delhi at the end, if at all.'

'Under what pretext should I meet these collectors and connoisseurs? What should our story be?'

'Oh, that is simple. You can mention that you are doing a research project under my guidance. You will send them a copy of the article when it is published. People like boasting about their collections when they are being interviewed for art journals and this should give you VIP access to their paintings.

'Let me make a few calls and organise some meetings in Kolkata. You can travel next week. Maybe I will come with you and show you some of the important art institutions in the city. We can do a city tour starting with the Government College of Arts and Craft and the Society of Oriental Arts. Thereafter we will visit the by lanes of the Kalighat Temples.'

'Kalighat Temples? Why is that relevant?'

'Jamini Roy was deeply influenced by the Kalighat Pats style of painting found in the bylanes of the temple. It will give you a feel of the city.'

The next week, Jay and Biswas made their first visit to Kolkata. They spent the first few days visiting different centres of art and culture in the city.

'Jay, you must absorb the atmosphere of the city, its culture, its people.'

'You must be joking, Biswas! You mean inhale the smoke and pollution in this overcrowded filthy city.'

'This city was not always like this, Jay. It was once the crown of the British Empire. Though it lost its political importance in 1911 when the capital of British India shifted to Delhi, it still remained an important centre for trade, commerce, art and culture. However, post-independence, it suffered from decades of economic stagnation with most of the trade and commerce shifting base to the city of Mumbai. Most of the families that you will be meeting over the next few days have enjoyed a position of prominence in the social circles of the old city.

'These families, unfortunately, shared their fortunes with the city they lived in. Like their city, their own financial position has declined with the passage of time and they are now far from their prime. Most of them are in urgent need of money, living in old dilapidated havelis which have seen better days and are now in complete ruins.

'However, their economic downfall has not rubbed off on their self-esteem and personal egos, which are still stuck in the past. They still live their lives recounting their past laurels, their discussions revolving around the accomplishments of their forefathers.

'Hence, any discussion regarding the sale of paintings has to be approached very carefully, otherwise you risk offending them and hurting their egos. In such a scenario, their hospitality will be short-lived and you risk being thrown out of their havelis even before you have the opportunity to finish your tea.

'Tomorrow, you will be meeting one of the most distinguished families in Kolkata, the Sarkars. Please be gentle with them, accord them all the respect and niceties they deserve. Best of luck!'

And with these pearls of wisdom, Biswas left for Mumbai.

The next day, Jay reached Mr Sarkar's haveli, or whatever was left of it. It must have been quite an imposing structure a few decades ago, he thought to himself. As he entered the living room with its high ceilings, he couldn't help but notice the broken chandeliers and the cobwebs on the wall.

Mr Sarkar was waiting to meet him in person.

'Sir, it is a pleasure to meet you. Thank you for granting me an audience at such a short notice. I seldom get an opportunity to meet someone belonging to such an accomplished family. Everyone in Kolkata seems to know you! If it wasn't for your family's patronage, fewer artists would have seen success in the present day.'

'Thank you for your kind words, Mr Malhotra. Can you shed light on the nature of your work and what brings you to Kolkata?'

'But of course, sir! As I mentioned to you on the phone, I am currently doing a research project on the Navaratnas under the mentorship of Mr Biswas Mukherjee. Mr Mukherjee speaks very highly of you and tells me that your private collection of Navaratnas can put that of many museums to shame.'

'He is a good man, Biswas. How is he doing? I haven't seen him for many years.'

'He is fine sir. In fact, he would have been here if it wasn't for an unforeseen engagement.' Now Jay cut to the chase. 'Sir, would it be possible for me to get a glimpse of your collection? Ever since you confirmed our meeting, I have been waiting for this moment, and now that it has finally arrived, I am finding it extremely difficult to hold back. I am sorry if I am inconveniencing you in any way,' he added apologetically.

'No, no, not at all. Let us proceed.'

The next two hours were spent critically evaluating the paintings, their composition, aesthetics, the formation of lines, brush movement and usage of colours.

'Sir, what an exceptional Jamini Roy! I have never seen anything like this.'

'Oh yes, this one is very rare. My father had purchased it from Jamini Roy himself. As you can see, it reflects a community event in a Santhal village. Santhals are the tribal community found in the interiors of Bengal and Odisha. Jamini Roy was deeply influenced by them and consequently, a large part of his oeuvre is dedicated to them.'

'Sir, I must compliment you on your taste and knowledge.'

'You are too kind, Mr Malhotra.'

Jay wanted to create a sense of camaraderie with Mr Sarkar. This would come in handy when he brought up the delicate subject of sales. Gradually, their discussions became much more casual, formality no longer in the air. Mr Sarkar began addressing him by his first name. He listened intently to Mr Sarkar's family stories, concurring and laughing with him much like a long-lost friend.

'Sir, what about the provenance of these paintings? Have they all been purchased from the artists?'

'Well, not every one of them, Jay, but almost all of them. Frankly, except for two paintings in this collection, all of them are primary purchases from the artists.'

'That is an exceptional record, sir.'

Now there was only one question that remained

unanswered: whether the paintings were available for sale. But this was the trickiest one. Had he done enough to get away with it without hurting Mr Sarkar's ego? Biswas' words kept reverberating in his mind; you must be delicate, very courteous, step back at the slightest hint of discomfort. He finally took a deep breath and spoke out.

'Sir, I am a little embarrassed to ask you this question. You see, my benefactor, who has funded this research project, is also a collector and has a keen interest in the paintings of the Navaratnas. While I am aware that the chances of an affirmative reply are extremely remote, I must ask you in complete confidence if any of these paintings are for sale.'

There was pindrop silence in the room. Had he broached the subject too early? Jay wondered.

'Sir, I apologise if I have hurt your feelings.'

This isn't too bad, he thought to himself. At least Mr Sarkar is still considering my offer, otherwise I would have been on the road by now. Maybe there is an opportunity to close a sale today.

As if to coax Mr Sarkar further, Jay said, 'Sir, if you concur, the payment will be on the spot.'

People reacted to his request to buy paintings in different ways. Some of them became offended and furious, questioning his motives and throwing him out of their houses. Then there were those who were much calmer in their approach, slowly absorbing and evaluating his offer, agreeing to the sale if it happened at a price of their liking and was done discreetly. Mr Sarkar belonged to this camp. He took a few days to come around but when he finally did, he did so in style, selling thirty paintings to him in a trot.

Jay called up Biswas, very excited.

'I have done it! Sarkar has been conquered. Thirty paintings on a trot, Biswas.'

'That's excellent, Jay. Frankly I didn't expect such a response. I have sent you a few other leads, please follow up on them. In particular, look up this Mahanalobis family.'

There was a major difference in the pricing of the paintings. They were far cheaper in Kolkata than their counterparts hanging in the galleries of Delhi and Mumbai. It was actually embarrassing to draw up a comparison between the two prices. Was this differential because Kolkata remained in a time warp and consequently, the rampant commercialisation prevalent in Delhi and Mumbai had not impacted it yet? Or was it because Jay had managed to purchase these paintings directly from the families, effectively cutting out the galleries and other middle men? Whatever the reason, it was to his benefit.

'How is it progressing, Jay?'

'It's progressing fine, Biswas,' replied Jay. 'Taking a little longer than I would have liked, but fine. By the way, did you get an opportunity to check the provenance of the paintings I had sent last month?'

Biswas could hear the excitement and confidence in his voice.

'Oh! Yes. They are all fine, impeccable actually.'

'Okay. Mahanalobis was a difficult nut to crack. I just managed a few from him. Roy and Chatterjee were much easier.'

'Keep at it. Let me know when you need more leads.'

'Send them anyway; it will keep me under pressure.'

Jay was an exceptional negotiator and deal-maker. On the one hand, he was courteous when approaching the delicate subject of the sale. However, his body language completely transformed the moment he got the slightest hint that the seller might be interested in his offer. He cut cheques on the spot, trying to conclude the sale immediately, knowing well that the decision to sell family heirlooms was extremely complex and difficult. There was a high probability that the seller would reverse his decision if he had too much time to mull over it. You had to strike while the iron was hot and conclude the sale immediately.

'Biswas, you haven't sent me any fresh leads over the past month!'

'Jay, I don't have any more leads to give you. You should conclude your work in Bengal and tie up all the loose ends. We should now commence work on phase two of our plan.'

'Okay. There are still a few of them on the list who haven't warmed up to me. Let me concentrate my efforts on them one last time.'

Even when he was thrown out of the house, Jay was relentless in his pursuit, leaving his contact details with a live offer before walking out. He had no personal ego or shame while pursuing a commercial objective; he could go back to the same person despite being mistreated by him if he felt there was even a glimmer of hope to conclude the deal. Sometimes it worked out and he got a call later in the day or the next day to come back and have a serious discussion. His persistence paid off more often than not in this game of cat and mouse. If he didn't receive a call, he called them back after a few days to apologise for his prior conduct, hoping for a reconciliation, only to pounce back with another offer.

It was hard work; some people were easier to crack than others and there were still those who did not relent. He made offers and counter-offers, followed by numerous rounds of meetings, dinners, lunches and whatever else it took to close the sale. After spending close to a year in Bengal, the first phase of his plan finally came to a close. He wasn't surprised by the results, which were exceptionally good. They had to be; after all, he had left nothing to chance. He had never failed an assignment in the past and there was no reason for him to do so now. Biswas, on the other hand, was elated with the results. He had not expected such a performance and was very impressed with Jay.

'Jay, we must celebrate our success before you commence work on the second phase.'

'Sorry, Biswas, but I don't intend on breaking the rhythm or momentum that we have created. We will take a break when all this is over. Please continue providing me with leads and guiding my effort.'

This fellow is a winner, Biswas thought to himself.

The modus operandi was the same in the second phase as earlier. He travelled to the erstwhile princely estates like Travancore, Hyderabad, Mysore, Baroda, Varanasi, Gwalior and Udaipur. These had been at the forefront of promoting art and culture and had provided patronage to many artists in the nineteenth and early twentieth century. He held numerous meetings on the pretext of carrying out a research assignment and met collectors, connoisseurs and gallery owners. He was successful in buying a number of Raja Ravi Varma's paintings in Travancore. Ravi Varma had won the patronage of many royal families like Mysore, Gwalior, Baroda and Jaipur by creating portraits and landscapes for his rich patrons while evolving his style in sync with the wishes of the royal people that he was visiting.

However, the effort to reward ratio was not the same as it had been in Bengal. He had to conduct a lot of meetings to buy the same number of paintings. He found that language was a constant barrier in the south, as some of the old families were not very fluent in English. Even when they did speak the English language, their thought process was in their native tongue. Due to this language barrier, he found it extremely difficult to build a camaraderie with them, which impacted his sales. He had a fleeting feeling that word had spread that he was acquiring paintings of the Navaratnas and hence a lot of people were holding back on their collections, hoping to ride the wave of increasing prices in the future. He had also heard in the passing a few times, that Patty had come calling, meeting some of the families. He wondered what she was up to. Was she looking at buying a few paintings herself to palm them off to him at a later date when the prices were higher?

Two years and hundreds of meetings later, he was finally reaching the end of his assignment to acquire the paintings of the Navaratnas. His consistent effort and perseverance had yielded exceptional results, netting him over 800 paintings of the old masters to add to his existing collection of 200 paintings, thereby taking his holdings to a grand total of over

1000 paintings. These paintings had been bought from people belonging to all walks of life, including fellow artists, art connoisseurs, gallery owners, families and relatives of artists, private collectors and journalists. He couldn't have achieved this success on his own and had depended on Biswas to reach out to his contacts. It was Biswas's network and goodwill in the art community that had helped open doors where there were none.

'Hello, Biswas. How are you? I am returning from Jaipur this weekend. We must celebrate.'

'Why, Jay?'

'This assignment is finally coming to an end.'

'How many did we manage?'

'Including the ones we already had, almost 1000.'

'That's great news. You have almost cornered a third of the market of the Navaratnas. However, there are still 2000 more out there.'

'Don't worry about them, Biswas. Some of them are lost. The remainder are part of distinguished collections and remain with close family and friends. I don't think they are going to be a problem any time soon.'

'You mean they will not sell them'.

'Not for the time being. However, I have a feeling that they will bite me in my arse once the prices have risen significantly.'

'So what do you propose?'

'I have left my contact details and will keep following up with them. I hope that my gallery will be the first port of call should they ever decide to part with their treasures.'

'That's excellent thinking, Jay. Let's catch up over the weekend.'

Jay had carefully documented the market of the Navaratnas and knew which collector or gallery held which specific piece. He firmly believed that in today's capitalist society, every piece of art was for sale; what was required was to find the right buyer who was willing to pay the price demanded by the seller.

Chapter 18

Rise of the Super Dealer

'Shall we open a bottle of champagne, Biswas?'

'You know I don't drink.'

'I thought you would make an exception tonight. After all, it is a special day.'

'I am sorry to be such a party pooper but I will gladly smoke a cigar with you. Somebody gifted me a box of Havanas which I have been preserving for such a moment.'

They both lit their cigars in unison and the sweet smell of the best leaf money could buy filled the bar. Jay yelled out to the waiter. 'Please get me a large Hibiki 30 on the rocks please.'

'So, what are you planning to do now?' Biswas asked.

'Nothing, actually. I am just going to relax for a few weeks, engage in some nocturnal adventures. I have been neglecting my social circle for far too long. What about you?'

Biswas laughed, 'Well, I have been contemplating delving into art restoration and authentication. You know that kind of work is close to my heart and will keep me excited. Now that this assignment is over, I can dedicate more time to it.'

'How did you come up with this idea?'

'I have been mulling over it for some time. The new millennium has seen a sudden surge of interest in Indian art. Hundreds of galleries with dubious backgrounds have mushroomed across the country, manned by people who have limited or no knowledge of art, supported by self-proclaimed experts whose scholarly works are unknown.'

'Hey, are you taking a pot shot at me?'

'No, not at all, but you will be surprised to know how bad things are. The art infrastructure in our country is insufficient to cope with this sudden rise in interest. You can literally count the number of institutions on your fingers which have put any concerted effort towards developing infrastructure and recording the evolution of art in India. Art forgery is a big problem facing the industry and I expect it to only increase in complexity in the coming years as the prices of contemporaries and masters rise at a feverish pace.'

'If it's that bad, how come I don't know about it?'

'It's a well-kept secret. Everyone is having a field day making money left, right and centre. No one wants to acknowledge the problem but that doesn't mean it doesn't exist. A mere look at history will tell you that such periods of exuberance are followed by a lot of pain and despair.'

'Stop. We need to change the topic, Biswas. I was on this nice high and I am losing the buzz in my head now.'

'I apologise for spoiling your mood. This is what happens when you converse with an art historian—we have no life outside our work. Let's have this discussion some other day. Tell me what's happening with you. I am sure you have more interesting things to talk about.'

'Well, I have been reading an autobiography of Larry Gagosian.'

'The art dealer?'

'Not just any art dealer, Biswas. Give the man the respect he deserves. He is a "Super Dealer", the largest and the most powerful in the world. They say his establishment has a revenue larger than the combined revenues of the two largest auction houses.'

'Oh! He's that big!'

'Yes, and what really excites me is the fact that he is a first-generation entrepreneur, comes from a humble family without any background in art. His father was a simple accountant; his mother a small-time movie actress, and to top it all he graduated from UCLA with a degree in English, not arts.'

Jay took a big swig of the Hibiki 30. 'Oh! This whisky is really good; the Japanese have the Scots in their kilts on a run.

'Art insiders agree that his biggest accomplishment is creating the posthumous market for mid- and late-career Warhols, defining them as a subcategory and consequently, exponentially raising their value.'

'Wow! So he is the guy behind Warhols.'

By now even Biswas, who didn't care much for the commercial aspects of the art industry, was listening keenly to Jay.

'Yes. They say that one day in 1985, while having lunch with Warhol at his studio, Gagosian came across several canvases full of abstract green and gold splotches, pools and metallic lines. Warhol called them his "piss paintings" because they had been created by urinating on wet oxidised copper paint.'

'What? Are you serious? This is crazy.'

'These paintings were old and no one had paid much attention to them. However, Gagosian differed in his opinion and saw an opportunity where others had seen only dirt. He saw large portions of Warhol's oeuvre being undervalued and convinced Warhol to allow him to showcase these works. He scanned Warhol's inventory and pulled out works which had been overlooked and then showcased them in an exhibition that identified them as an important body of work when put together.

'Biswas, today the Warhol market is the backbone of the contemporary art market in the world and by some estimates accounts for a fifth of the value of the contemporary art market. If the Warhol market sneezes, the market for contemporaries catches a cold. Do you see the similarities? Gagosian did to Warhol what we have set out to do to the Navaratnas. I am reading about him to identify the traits which have made him so successful. I think there is so much I can learn from him. Why was he successful when so many before him failed?'

'And, have you figured out any of these traits?'

'Yes, I have identified a few. He has the biggest names in the money management world as his clients. You can question the credentials of these money managers as patrons of high culture and art, but no one can doubt their acumen when it comes to making sound investment decisions. In short, he has big money riding on him. But that is not all. He also represents the careers and estates of the world's top artists, sixty to seventy of them. He is known to poach artists from rival galleries once their market has matured and is poised to explode. And he has this uncanny ability to source paintings which are supposedly not available. This ensures that the biggest museums, collectors, investors and connoisseurs keep him in good humour despite his arrogance and often aggressive behaviour.

'That's very interesting. Keep up the good work. I hope you find the information you are looking for.'

'And one more thing. Much like me, he has a keen eye and knows an opportunity when he sees one. I am telling you, Biswas, we are on the right track. The entire art fraternity will sing our praises in times to come as the people behind the resurgence of the Navaratnas.'

'I am sure they will, Jay. It's getting late now. Let's call it a night.'

'I will pay you a visit next week, Biswas. I want to know more about your future plans.'

'Sure, just give me a call.'

≈

Chapter 19

Chaos Rules Art Authentication

B iswas was busy watering the plants in his small terrace garden. He liked spending mornings tending to his plants. It was his way of relaxing. Earlier, he had received a phone call from Jay who had invited himself to his house. He looked at his watch; it was already ten in the morning. Jay should be arriving at any moment.

He wondered why Jay was so inquisitive about his future plans. Suddenly, the bell rang and he went downstairs to open the front door. It being a Sunday, his house help was on leave.

As Jay entered the living room, the strong aroma of filter coffee filled his nostrils. This was a pleasant change from the smell of stale cigar smoke that usually greeted him in this house. He took a long deep sniff and then asked Biswas for a cup of coffee. 'Of course, I put it to brew the moment I received your call.'

After taking a few hurried sips of the coffee, Jay said, 'Let us continue our conversation of the previous week. I remember cutting you off rather unceremoniously midway through your sentence.'

'I will start afresh since I don't completely recall where we ended our discussion. You had mesmerised me with your story about Gagosian.'

'That wasn't a story, those were facts.'

'Well, as I was telling you the other evening, art authentication assumes greater importance in a country where the corresponding art infrastructure is insufficient, as the gaps in infrastructure are exploited by the underground forgery market.'

'Yup, that makes sense. So when are you planning to start your new work?'

'That's the problem, Jay; it is easier said than done. I don't know where to start as globally, art authentication itself is in complete disarray. Over the past few decades, it has fallen into increasing disrepute, associated with vested interests and manipulation of the market.'

'Hold on, Biswas. I didn't understand a single word of what you just said. Can you please explain in layman's terms?'

'There are different methodologies which can be deployed for authenticating a painting. Provenance research, visual and stylistic analysis, are based on the old world of connoisseurship. Pigment analysis, X-ray/infrared analysis and so on come under what is called scientific analysis. These methodologies give rise to various forms of evidence and data which then needs to be analysed and interpreted to arrive at a final conclusion. The problem plaguing art authentication today is that there are no standards. It's totally unregulated. The art community is trying very hard to establish standards but there is no professional control. You can shop around for a scientific report that probably corroborates what you want.'

'So are you telling me that the data or the evidence can be easily manipulated to arrive at any result you want?'

'Yes, broadly speaking, you can say that. Manipulation is possible because the collective profession's approach is chaotic. Documentation, scientific analysis and judgement by eye are used and ignored opportunistically by people who have vested interests in arriving at varying results. The process is very selective, not all evidence is relied upon to arrive at the final conclusion. Generally, only high-quality secure evidence is considered whereas others are discarded. The various kinds of evidence, their status and what job they do in proving the case are never really inspected.

'Further, owners and investors are commissioning tests on pictures with a "visual plausibility" clause that allows them to censor data that is not consistent with their case. If, for example, a report casts doubt on a Van Gogh attribution because tests reveal a pigment only developed after the artist's death, contracts prevent the report's author from speaking about the findings and the information is suppressed.'

'Holy shit! Are you serious? What about scientific analysis? Science can't lie.'

'No, science doesn't lie. However, it can only deliver non-arbitrary data in relation to a specific query but this data still needs interpretation to arrive at the correct result. Technical examination is very complicated and depends on a host of factors such as the nature of equipment, settings and skills of its operators. Any slight change in the condition can give differing results.

'The art world doesn't fully comprehend the parameters of scientific examination, what it can and cannot deliver. Even when adequately understood, there is no accepted way to integrate scientific analysis into other historical analyses, including judgement by the eye. The different bodies of evidence too often appear incommensurable. Further, the results obtained by scientific examination tend only to tell us that there is nothing in the way of an attribution rather than providing positive arguments.'

'So what do you plan to do, Biswas?'

'I plan to attack this problem at two levels. First and foremost, I will get a few like-minded experts together to deal with the problem of forgeries in the art market by establishing a centre for carrying out art authentication. I can take the lead on Tagore, someone else on Jamini Roy, someone for Nandalal Bose and so on. Second, we will impart professional training on documentation and establishing provenance. This will allow us to create some consensus and standards in dealing with different forms of evidence.'

'But why does it have to be you? This is not your problem.'

'I am an elder of this industry. If I don't do it, who will? After all, we all have a responsibility to the industry which gives us our livelihood.'

'Okay, but others seem to be busy making money. These problems don't seem to be impacting them.'

'It will impact us all, Jay, it's just a matter of time. By the way, why are you so worried about what I propose to do?'

'Because I still need you to help me out with the marketing of the Navaratnas to the key influencers in the art industry, the museums and connoisseurs. Our work is only half done.'

'Oh! That's why you have been losing sleep. Don't worry; I will be available whenever you need my help. I understand my commitments, you need not worry.'

Biswas could see the relief on Jay's face.

'Here, have another mug of hot coffee. Go back home and relax for a few weeks. When you want to start, give me a shout. We will first have to catalogue all the paintings in your inventory in order of their importance. Only then can we commence with the marketing.'

≈

Chapter 20

The Influencers are the Key

Creating a market for an artist or a group of artists was easier said than done. It required persistence, patience and money. It couldn't be achieved overnight and once achieved, it would have to be constantly reinforced. Luckily for Jay, he was gifted with all these virtues.

The evolution of a new artist was similar to the acceptance curve for a new product; his work was first examined and accepted by the trendsetters, who in turn influenced the early adopters who were then blindly followed by the market at large. The museums were the trendsetters in the art industry. Their actions were closely examined by the art connoisseurs and collectors who were interested in deciphering emerging trends and artists. The art connoisseurs and collectors were the early adopters who influenced the purchase decisions of the larger art fraternity, including dealers, gallery owners and investors.

However, before he could commence with the marketing,

it was essential that he take the necessary steps to keep the size of his existing holdings a secret. This information was only available to two people, him and Biswas, and he planned to keep it that way. To this end, he had rented a warehouse, its existence off the books of the gallery. He planned to keep the inventory of the Navaratnas at this warehouse and gradually transfer them to the warehouse of the gallery, depending on the demand and supply situation in the market.

Meanwhile, Biswas worked diligently at cataloguing the existing inventory of the Navaratnas. They had decided that the paintings would be divided into three categories, A, B and C. Category A would consist of the top fifty paintings in the collection, the most prized possessions, to be sold very selectively in limited quantities to the top museums, connoisseurs and once in a while, at auctions to create new benchmarks. Category B would consist of paintings falling in the top quartile and category C would consist of the remainder.

After a fortnight, he received a call from Biswas, informing him that the cataloguing of the paintings was complete.

'You should reach out to the museums now and fix up meetings with their curators.'

'But why the curators? I thought they had an acquisition committee?'

'Yes they do, consisting of the curator, artists, experts and members of the board of trustees. However, the curator is central to the acquisition process, responsible for identifying new works to be acquired by the museum. He creates an internal note on the provenance of the work and circulates the same amongst the members of the acquisition committee for discussion. Based on his recommendation and collective decision-making, the acquisition committee decides whether the work should be acquired or not. Hence in order to break into the museums, it is essential to win over the support of their curators.'

'Okay. I will do that first thing in the morning, Biswas. But do you think they will bite the bullet?'

'We are likely to face some initial resistance.'

'Why, don't they know about the Navaratnas?'

'Of course they do, Jay. Anyone associated with Indian art knows about the Navaratnas. Their brand is well recognised by the museums and connoisseurs.'

'Then what is the problem?'

'There is a perception in the art community that the best works created by the Navaratnas were acquired by the government in the early 1970s and consequently, what remains in the market are artworks that do not showcase the depth of the artists' oeuvre and are therefore, not worthy of inclusion in the collections of the top museums.'

'Biswas, you are also an expert. What do you think? You have seen all the paintings in the collection. What is your view?'

'I think we have some outstanding pieces in our collection, worthy of any museum in the country. The government action in the 1970s was limited in its scope; it simply identified some of the most important collections of the Navaratnas held in private hands and acquired them. However, their action was not comprehensive; they didn't go looking very hard to identify people who had a single masterpiece hanging on their living room walls like you did. After evaluating your collection, I have the confidence to say that their perception is incorrect. However, the larger art fraternity does not have the advantage of my knowledge, they have not seen what I have and thus I expect them to be sceptical in the beginning. We will have to work on them to win them over to our side.'

'In that case, Biswas, let me reach out to a few museums and see how they respond. If I feel that I am not getting anywhere, I will request you to intervene.'

A fortnight later, Jay called Biswas. It was late in the evening and he was a couple of whiskies down.

'Boss, I need your help!'

'What happened? How far did you get? Did you manage any meetings?'

'Meetings? How do I get a meeting if these buggers don't even answer my calls?'

'They aren't taking your calls?'

'They were till I told them that I wanted to meet them regarding the Navaratnas. Then the line suddenly went cold. Since then I have managed to reach only their voice mails and on a few days, their secretaries. I think even the secretaries are getting bored of me now.'

'Where are you right now?'

'Getting drunk at a bar with a thirty-something secretary. I am getting desperate, Biswas. I need these meetings.'

'Don't worry. I will make the calls tomorrow morning and revert to you. Now go back home and sleep well.'

'Are you sure I don't need to take this woman home with me?'

Jay could hear loud laughter on the other side of the phone.

'Not for the meeting, you don't. Otherwise it's your call.'

'Oh! Thank God. That's a relief. She says she is in love with me. Speak with you tomorrow.'

Biswas called one of the curators the next day.

'Jigan Bhai, how are you? This is Biswas Mukherjee.'

'Arrey sir, it is a pleasure to hear your voice. What makes you call my humble office?'

'I need a favour of you, Jigan.'

'Hukum, sahib!'

'A friend of mine, Jay Malhotra, has been trying to reach you. I will be obliged if you can give him a meeting.'

'Jay Malhotra? Is that the same chap who was talking about the Navaratnas?'

'Yes, that's him.'

'Very persuasive this chap Malhotra is, sir. My secretary reminds me every day in the morning to give him a meeting but I have been avoiding him. You know, sir, all the good works by the Navaratnas were acquired by the government long ago. I told this fellow that he should visit the National Gallery of Modern Art at Delhi if he wants to refresh his memory.'

'Jigan, I know what you are saying, but give him a meeting. I have seen his collection with my own eyes and can assure you that it will be time well spent.'

'What, you have seen the works with your own eyes and are excited?'

'Yes.'

'All right, I will fix the meeting for the coming Friday but no commitments, boss, you understand that, right?'

'Yes, yes, no commitments, just a meeting. I will accompany him.'

'Great! See you then.'

Biswas fixed up two more meetings with the leading museums by mid-afternoon and called up Jay.

'Wake up, Jay! I have fixed meetings with the top three museums.'

'How did you manage it?'

'It's not important. We have five days to get our act together. I have given them my word. Meet me in the evening with the catalogue of the paintings. Let us sit down and decide on the paintings that we will show them.'

And so they did, eight paintings from the collection of the top fifty, a mix of Tagores, Jamini Roys and Nandalal Boses.

'Jay, these paintings reflect the depth and breadth of our collection. I will email you my thoughts on these paintings; use this information along with your own notes on their provenance to create a presentation. First impressions are very important and you don't get a second opportunity to make them.'

They arrived at the museum half an hour before time and were immediately guided to a private viewing room located in the non-public area. The paintings were hung on the wall and simultaneously, all the lights in the room other than those highlighting the first painting were switched off. This is the way Biswas wanted it. He felt that this would create a melodramatic effect, keeping the attention of the curator focused on the painting being discussed. After Jay had concluded his presentation and taken questions, they would gradually move towards the second painting. At that moment, Biswas would instruct the museum staff to turn on the display lights.

The curator entered the room at half past ten a.m. sharp.

'I have a meeting at half past eleven, Biswas babu,' he announced. 'Get me a magnifying glass!' he yelled to his staff. 'Please continue with your presentation, Mr Malhotra. It might seem to you that my attention is elsewhere but I can assure you that I am listening to every word coming out of your mouth.'

Jay finished his five-minute presentation quickly and asked the curator if he had any questions. He got no response. The curator seemed to be in a trance, mesmerised by the work that was in front of him. After about two minutes of silence, the curator started firing questions one after the other. He looked excited, much like a ten-year-old is when presented with his favourite toy. The questions were never-ending; every now and then Jay would glance at his watch, the minute hand ticking away. He was sweating profusely by now. How the hell was he supposed to complete the presentation in time when they had spent almost forty-five minutes in front of the first painting?

As if reading his thoughts, Biswas told him to calm down. When they finally moved towards the second painting, the curator called out to his secretary, 'Please cancel my meetings for the day, I am not to be disturbed.' Jay was visibly relieved. They ended the meeting at five in the evening with a small lunch break in between. It was a marathon event; Jay was completely drained, his voice hoarse from the constant speaking. He figured he must have answered a few hundred questions, maybe more. Biswas looked composed; he had been through similar meetings in the past. By the time they left the museum, the curator could no longer hold back his excitement. He took Biswas to a corner and begged him not to showcase the paintings anywhere else.

'Go home and rest, Biswas babu,' he said, 'Why would you go anywhere else? I will buy them, the whole lot. I need one week to get the approval of my acquisition committee. You know how it works. If I could cut a cheque on my own, you would have it by now.'

Biswas gave him no comfort, telling him that he could only advise Jay and that the final decision was his to make.

Over the next week, they met the curators of the remaining museums. Their responses were similar.

Within a fortnight of these meetings, there was a bidding war between the top three museums to acquire the paintings. While none of them showed their desperation to Jay, they were much more candid about their precarious position in front of Biswas, whom they considered as one of their own and constantly hounded him.

'Boss, for old time's sake, you have to manage this Jay Malhotra fellow. I need those paintings.'

'What do you mean? It might be difficult.'

'I have already committed to the board of trustees that we will have them in our gallery by the end of the week. Don't put me in such a precarious position, boss.'

'This is embarrassing. At least tell me that I can have a few if not all.'

Every other day, Biswas called Jay with a new offer or a counter-offer.

'I am not interested in their monetary compensation, Biswas! How do they rank in terms of prestige and reputation?'

'Frankly, there isn't much difference. They are all the same. Depending on whom you ask, you will get different results.'

'Well, in that case, ask them for other benefits and concessions.'

'Like what?'

'Marketing concessions, credit to our gallery, right to exhibit and so on.'

And so a deal was struck for the eight paintings on the following terms:

i) The paintings would be immediately put on public display.

ii) They would be displayed in the Central Hall or another place of prominence, surrounded by the best works of the old masters and contemporaries in the possession of the museum.

iii) They would be part of all exhibitions held by the museum for a period of twelve months from the date of purchase.

Needless to say, Jay would be at liberty to disclose the names of these museums to the media and count them in his esteemed client list.

Now that the top three museums were on board, it was a cake walk to get the remaining ones on his side. Word was immediately out about the new purchases in the exclusive art fraternity—there was a new gallery in town dealing in the

Navaratnas and Biswas Mukherjee had significant influence on its owner.

The odds had changed and Jay didn't have to lift a finger. They came to him one after the other, looking for what he had to offer. They were no longer sceptical about the resurgence of the Navaratnas, their questions centred on the paintings themselves and their provenance. He found them understanding, their body language subdued. It was almost as if they had accepted their fate. The new trend had been set by the top three and the rest followed them blindly.

Much to his surprise, he hadn't heard from the art connoisseurs or collectors. Surely, they must have heard about the new trend by now, he thought. Biswas had mentioned to him that they had their eyes and ears planted in the museums. In some cases, they knew decisions even before they were made by the board of trustees. Where were they? he wondered.

Unknown to him, there was frenzied activity in the circle of the connoisseurs and collectors. Their sources in the acquisition committee immediately informed them of the new purchases the museums had made. Their first reaction was one of complete disbelief, some of them even questioning the source of information. The purchase of Navaratnas was so out of the ordinary, it had the potential to spoil the harmony in the art fraternity. Over the last two decades, all of them, including the museums, had invested heavily in the contemporaries; there was comfort in togetherness, in knowing that you were part of the herd. However, these new purchases suggested otherwise. They were ad hoc, or did they signify something far greater, perhaps a change in the trend itself?

They needed more information to make a decision. They went about collating the same, reaching out to their contacts in the museums, present curators, ex-curators, experts and so on. As soon as they became aware that the top ten museums in the country had made similar purchases, it dawned on them that the trend had changed. What followed was complete mayhem.

It was a Sunday afternoon when Jay received the first call. This was followed by half a dozen others. Up till then he had been under the illusion that he possessed a private number which was not accessible to the public at large. This delusion met its end in minutes.

He knew the moment he took the call that he was speaking to someone important and powerful. The tone was unmistakable, controlled but authoritative. The person on the other end didn't care that he had called him on a Sunday afternoon on his private number. He seemed to be someone who was used to his calls being answered and it didn't matter which day of the week it was. Jay was fine with this attitude. This was business after all, and there were no holidays in the life of a successful art dealer.

He pampered them and allowed himself to be bullied.

'Of course, Mr Nafatlal. I know about you. Your family needs no introduction in Mumbai.'

'Where is your gallery located, Mr Malhotra? Fort? Did you just say that the gallery is located at Fort? I must confess that I haven't heard about you. Which gallery did you say you worked for in the past? You were an investment banker! New to the art fraternity, I see. I heard you recently sold a few paintings of the Navaratnas to the museums.'

'Yes, sir, you are well informed,' Jay smiled.

'Should you have any more of the same provenance, I would be most interested in looking at them.'

'Sure, sir, I will organise a private viewing for you at the gallery.'

Chapter 21

Time to Make a Splash

'Good morning, Jay. How are things progressing? I haven't heard from you lately.'

'Things are going according to plan, Biswas. I have the key influencers in my pocket.'

'That's great. By the way, I was recently the chief guest at an art exhibition in Kolkata. I was pleasantly surprised to see a few Navaratnas there.'

'Oh yes, we have invested a lot in marketing and PR. I have a full-time team working behind the scenes to ensure that they get adequate exposure at exhibitions and art fairs. We even sponsored some of those exhibitions. Did you find them well represented?'

'Yes, they were placed amongst the best of the contemporaries.'

'You mean with the Husains and Razas.'

'Yes. Was this what you expected?'

'Yes. I want people to place the Navaratnas in the same

category as the popular contemporaries which command high prices. Once this association is complete and they have their own following, I will push for solo exhibitions.'

'Okay. What else are you up to these days?'

'I am investing in the backend, Biswas. Drop by the gallery some day; you will see a lot of new faces. I intend on making a big splash at the auctions scheduled for later this year.'

'Will do, Jay. Take care.'

Jay's marketing team was working overtime to coordinate its efforts with those of a leading PR agency to ensure that the exhibitions showcasing the Navaratnas received adequate coverage in both the print and television media. In addition to providing background material and relevant research to different journalists covering the art sector, they would plant stories about the rise of the Navaratnas across the print and social media. Several articles appeared in the dailies, highlighting the recent purchase of Navaratnas by the leading museums in the country. Jay ensured that the curators who played a central role in these purchases were given their due opportunity to shine in front of the media.

These marketing activities helped create an aura around the paintings of the Navaratnas and simultaneously elevated Jay into an art insider, someone who was regularly quoted and celebrated as a kingmaker in the art fraternity. He was the newest rising star and was flooded with invitations to gallery launches, exhibitions, auctions and cocktail parties.

He was in the thick of it all and with acquaintances becoming long-lost friends, he could no longer do or say anything wrong. People followed his every move, listened attentively to every word he said. Life was suddenly good and it was easy for him to lose focus. He was already weary of this newfound attention and fame. The women were the most difficult to handle, always getting inside his pants. But slowly and steadily, he settled into his larger-than-life stature.

He was now an insider in the exclusive art circle, an influencer who could dictate the tastes of those around him. He was extended the same niceties as the rest of the group. They functioned on the principle of exclusion; once you became an insider, you excluded the others on the basis of your intellectual and cultural capital.

He ran into Patty at one of these parties. He hadn't met her since their last interaction a few years earlier when he had been thrown out of her house. Now the tide had turned. He was the kingmaker who could do no wrong and she was no longer the queen she used to be. But as far as her appearance went, she still looked hot.

'Enjoying your newfound fame, Jay Malhotra?' she asked.

Jay just smiled without saying a word. This pissed her off and she went into a rage.

'You bastard, you stole my idea, expert and paintings!'

'You are such a sore loser, Patty. Just to set the record straight, I purchased the paintings and Biswas joined me on his own, disgusted with his past employment. In regard your idea, it was just that…an idea which had failed in your hands. And don't you lecture me on morality, bitch; you used me like a toy in front of your friends, shining in the glory of your latest trophy. I just learnt from the best and executed it perfectly. Don't get upset now, we are part of the same fraternity and will be meeting often.'

'Your rise has been extremely steep and so will your fall. It will be one of your new "friends" who will push you off the cliff,' she said viciously.

What the hell she is talking about wondered Jay. Is she up to something that I don't know about.

They ended the discussion by kissing each other good night for the benefit of the fraternity watching them.

The time had finally come for him to create a big splash by participating in an auction. Jay had worked diligently to consolidate his position in the market, investing heavily in the brand of the Navaratnas. It was time to set the public benchmarks on fire, to exploit and enjoy the fruits of the brand that he had successfully created. Until now, he had limited his sales to the connoisseurs and collectors. These sales had been made discreetly through the gallery. While there was a consensus in the market that there was a revival in the demand for the Navaratnas, no one knew how strong the demand was or the extent to which the prices had moved.

He took out two of the finest paintings in his private collection and made them available to an auction house for sale on an anonymous basis. One of them was a masterpiece by Jamini Roy while the other was a piece by Raja Ravi Varma. One thing he was certain of was that these two paintings would be vehemently contested, having received queries in the past from several museums and collectors. However, he had held on to them for this moment, to create a buzz, to set a new auction record.

Unknown to anyone else, he had also lined up a few

friendly parties to push up the prices in case the demand for the paintings fell short of expectation. However, no such friendly support was required on the day of the auction. Instead, a bidding war ensued between a museum and an art collector for the Ravi Varma, the collector eventually being adjudged the victor when the museum had run out of its allocated budget for the painting. In the process, the Ravi Varma had created an auction record, selling at a 150 per cent premium over its reserve price. Though the results for the Jamini Roy were not as dramatic, it also ended up setting a new auction record.

The results were being closely monitored by the entire investor community and as soon as they were out, there was a complete frenzy in the art market to acquire paintings by the Navaratnas. All those people who had been sitting on the fence decided to take the plunge into the market. No one wanted to miss the bus, the new trend in the art market.

Biswas tried reaching Jay on his mobile phone several times to congratulate him on the auction results. Finally, he managed to reach Jay's secretary, who passed the phone to Jay.

'Congratulations, Jay! Where have you been? I have been trying to reach you since the morning.'

'Sorry, Biswas, I had to switch off my phone. I have been getting calls since the morning. Everyone wants these paintings and I mean everyone: the politicians, Bollywood, everyone. We had to delay the gallery opening in the morning. We were worried about crowd control and had to call the cops.'

'Are things sorted out now?'

'Yeah, it's all sorted out. By the way, we sold ten paintings today, more than we sold over the entire month. And that's not counting the hundreds of queries we have received on the phone, which I am sure will result in a few more sales. We are having a dream run, Biswas.'

'Great job! Keep it up, Jay.'

Yeah, the time has come to cream the market, Jay thought as he hung up.

≈

Chapter 22

It's Raining Money!

The next four years witnessed an unprecedented rise in the prices of the Navaratnas with many of them reaching the million-dollar mark. This exuberance was reflective of the success Jay Malhotra had achieved in creating the perfect investment environment for the Navaratnas.

Jay's understanding of the dynamics of the market was second to none. Prior to joining the art industry, he had successfully manipulated the capital markets to make a financial killing for himself and his clients. He understood the psyche of the investor and how to exploit it. He knew that if the predominant factor driving the purchase decision of a painting was its investment value, then investor behaviour or how he responded to a rise or fall in the price of a painting could be broadly predicted.

Investors were not always logical and rational in their purchase decisions and were thus open to exploitation. According to the economic theory of demand and supply, any increase in the price of a product would have automatically reduced its demand while increasing its supply, thereby resulting in an equilibrium when the two became equal. However, a sudden sharp increase in the price of an asset could have quite the opposite effect, restricting the supply from existing investors while simultaneously increasing the demand from new investors.

When the price of an asset rose sharply, existing investors reduced sales in anticipation of higher prices whereas investors who had been sitting on the fence hoping for prices to decline rushed in to buy the asset out of fear that it would rise further. By this logic, prices should have increased indefinitely. However, this was not true, as sustained periods of a price rise created bubbles and eventually lead to crashes in the market. Because it was often difficult to observe intrinsic values in real life markets, bubbles were often conclusively identified only in retrospect, when a sudden drop in prices appeared.

In order to prevent the formation of bubbles followed by periods of doom in the market, it was essential to ensure that the rise in prices was gradual with regular periods of rest or consolidation. These periods of consolidation resulted in a healthy churn by allowing new investors to enter and existing investors to exit the market.

By following the above rules, it was possible to manipulate the prices of any asset class, including art. Jay had amassed almost a third of all existing Navaratnas in private hands and subsequently exercised a strong control over the supply in the market. By managing the supply and keeping it less than the corresponding demand, he was able to ensure a stable price rise in the market. However, it was essential to contain any sudden changes in demand or supply.

He maintained a detailed database of investors who had purchased paintings from his gallery. By comparing their purchase price with the benchmark price prevalent in the market, he was able to calculate how much profit they were earning on their investment. The behaviour of an investor who was sitting on large unrealised profit was difficult to predict as his temptation to sell the artwork was higher than someone who had less profit or no profit at all and consequently, could be a source of supply in the market. Hence, in order to maintain decorum and stability, it was essential to provide an exit to such investors during periods of consolidation in favour of new investors. Similarly, every time the markets became hot, that is the prices rose too fast, Jay would increase the supply of artwork to absorb additional demand and restore equilibrium.

Investors strongly preferred avoiding losses to acquiring gains. According to some studies, losses were twice as powerful psychologically as gains. Hence, every time an investor bought artwork at a higher acquisition cost, it could be safely presumed that he was not going to sell it so long as the price of the artwork remained at the same or lower level than his purchase price. By continuously introducing new investors into the market of the Navaratnas at higher prices, Jay ensured that at any given time there weren't any large sellers in the market.

Since all sales at the gallery were private, differential pricing could have been applied, depending on the utility of the client. A client who was a regular investor and who played by the rules of the gallery, that is, invested for the long term, didn't flip the artwork regularly and came back to the gallery to seek assistance in finding a buyer was given priority on both availability of artworks as well as pricing. Differential pricing was possible in the art industry because no two paintings were alike and also because all sales through galleries took place in utmost secrecy.

However, prices had to be closely monitored at auctions, which were beyond the control of the galleries and sites where any individual could participate in the buying process. Since the buyer was unknown, behaviour was difficult to ascertain. Further, auction results were public and thus set the benchmarks for how the artist was performing in the market. Hence it was essential to manage the auction prices by rigging the bidding process. Every time a new benchmark had been set at the auction for a particular artist, Jay decided, based on the demand situation prevalent in the market, how many paintings he wanted to sell at that price.

By continuously setting higher benchmarks at the auctions by rigging the bidding process, managing the supply to ensure it remained less than the corresponding demand and providing for periods of consolidation resulting in a healthy churn of investors in the market, Jay was able to successfully manipulate the markets of the Navaratnas to new highs.

It was smooth sailing in the first two years when the Navaratnas were highly under-owned and Jay exercised strict control over their supply. However, as both the prices and ownership increased, the markets became more volatile and difficult to manage.

He was now regularly receiving queries from existing

investors who wanted to take advantage of the high prices and exit the market. As a result, his sales team was looking for ever larger numbers of new investors to absorb the supply from existing investors. Only once this supply had been satiated, could Jay hope to sell paintings from his inventory, otherwise he risked declining prices which could have easily set a panic in the market.

His marketing team was burning the midnight oil, organising new art fairs and exhibitions in their effort to attract new investors. However, despite their best efforts, an ever smaller number of paintings was being sold from the gallery. It was essential to provide an exit to all investors and maintain liquidity in the market. Not doing so could have created distressed sales and a crash in the corresponding prices.

Increasingly, Jay was being forced to either buy the paintings on his own account (obviously this was not known to the investors) or rig the bidding prices even higher at auctions to reduce the supply of paintings coming into the market. Neither of these courses was good for the gallery. Jay knew this, but unfortunately, it had to be done, and there was no other way out.

He had to find a solution and it had to be done fast. He was running out of liquidity, the most important factor for maintaining investor confidence.

≈

Chapter 23

Five Per Cent and She's Yours

'Who can I approach? The usual suspects, investors and art collectors have already been tapped. The exhibitions and art fairs are helpful, but their impact is too slow and small. This market needs an immediate shot of liquidity to turn the cycle and remove the sluggishness. But who can provide such liquidity?'

The answer to these questions evaded him, leaving him restless and irritated.

'Fuck! I can't go through this again, not after coming so far ahead on the road. Now is the time for me to enjoy the fruits of the sapling I had sowed years back.'

And just when he thought that things couldn't get any worse, the housing bubble burst in the United States, resulting in the collapse of several multi-billion dollar financial institutions, including Lehman Brothers. This event was a major sentiment damper and rattled the global economy. Funds were moved overnight from risky assets to the traditional safe havens of cash and gold. Bonds, equities, real estate and art crashed globally.

Interestingly, the impact on the Indian economy was rather muted; it was resilient to the global shock because it wasn't leveraged. Temperamentally, Indian consumers were risk-averse with low levels of borrowing and high rates of saving. Further, the large parallel cash economy in India acted as a buffer to absorb the financial shock.

However, Jay could see the tell-tale signs of an imminent crash in the art market in India. The transactions were drying up. Liquid assets such as bonds and equity exhibited a transparent market where the price immediately adjusted to changes in the underlying market. However, this was not possible in the case of art and real estate, which had an opaque market. During periods of slowdown, the transaction volume dried up in the case of such assets. This was because buyers and sellers were still trying to appraise the impact of the slowdown on the price of the underlying asset. The sellers still felt that they should get a better price than that being offered by the buyers, whereas the buyers were looking at the corresponding crash in liquid assets like stocks and bonds and accordingly adjusted their offers.

With low transaction volumes, even one large distressed seller could easily create a bloodbath in the market. He could singlehandedly crash the market by tens of per cent.

'Oh my God,' Jay thought. 'We are looking at mayhem in the market. I have to find a solution. I have to double my efforts to find new investors and get more out of the existing ones.'

Jay went on an overdrive for the next fortnight, flogging his sales team, holding review meetings to evaluate the sales effort, daily call records and monitor the pipelines of prospective clients.

This pressure didn't help his cause one bit; instead, it forced many of his best performing employees to resign in disgust. Instead of improving the sales numbers, his plan backfired. He should have known better: he was selling art, not tomatoes at the local vegetable mandi.

Shocked by the mass exodus of his tenured employees, he called for an open forum to address them.

'I apologise to you all; I have screwed up and I shouldn't have put you through such pressure. We are reverting to the earlier system with immediate effect. I will make personal calls to our colleagues who have quit over the past month and request them to rejoin. I also want to have a brainstorming session to come up with ideas on how to improve our productivity. Does anyone have any suggestions?'

Only one person raised her hand.

'Yes, you at the back, please speak up.'

'Sir, in the past we refused to entertain clients who were not to our liking, people we felt were in it for the short run, would flip the paintings regularly, especially at auctions. We should open the flood gates and accept them all.'

'Excellent idea. Get working on it immediately.'

While his employees went back to working on the filth of the market, selling paintings to those who were considered degenerate, he continued picking his brains to find a long-term solution.

And then he woke up in the middle of the night. Eureka! He had the answer; it had been in front of him all this time, staring him in the face. It was time he did a rendezvous with his ex-boss, Samir Aggarwal, the banker. He had had a solution to every problem in the commercial world; the word 'impossible' didn't exist in his dictionary. Everything was possible, for the right price.

The demand for Navaratnas was slowing down and the market was becoming sluggish—this was a fact known to very few industry insiders. As far as the rest of the world was concerned, the Navaratnas were among the best-performing subcategories in the art market, having more than tripled in value over the past few years.

With such an impressive track record, Samir could surely find a few suckers to buy the story.

Jay couldn't sleep out of sheer excitement and anticipation. He was restless, tossing and turning repeatedly.

Finally, unable to take it anymore, he got out of bed. It was only four in the morning.

'What the hell!' he thought. 'Let me get working on the marketing collateral. I need to make an impact on that son of a bitch; otherwise he will see through my façade and know immediately that I am in deep shit.'

At nine, he called Samir Aggarwal to fix up a meeting.

'Jay, it is good to hear from you. I keep hearing every now and then that you have been making a lot of waves in the art industry. So tell me how I can help you.'

'Thanks, Samir,' replied Jay. 'I can't speak on the phone but I have an interesting proposition to discuss with you. Can we catch up for a quick drink sometime?'

'Let's meet at seven in the evening at the regular haunt. I need to be somewhere at half past eight.'

'Sure Samir, see you then.'

The regular haunt was a bar located in front of Jay's erstwhile office at Fort, Mumbai. You never knew who you might run into there. It was frequented by the big corporate bankers, the tycoons of Dalal Street and the occasional industrialist. Jay hadn't visited the bar ever since he had been expelled from the capital markets. He felt a little uncomfortable going there and running into people from his earlier life.

He reached the bar at seven to find his erstwhile boss at a table already.

'Hey, good to see you, Jay. You haven't gained a pound since I saw you last. Still running the marathon, are you? I hope there are no hard feelings for what happened in the past; we did what was required to protect the firm. You understand, right?'

'Yes, boss, no hard feelings. Life is so fast-paced, who has the time to worry about the past?'

'Now that's my boy. I took the liberty of ordering a lager for you.'

Jay took a few long sips of the beer. Then he looked up at Samir, who was examining him closely, trying to read his mind.

'Let's cut to the chase, Jay. What business did you want to discuss?'

Jay began his well-rehearsed speech.

'Samir, as you are aware, I have been associated with the art industry for a while. The past few years have been exceptional; we have seen an unprecedented bull run with prices of both contemporaries and old masters increasing exponentially. This, in my opinion, is reflective of the maturing tastes of Indian investors. This is only the tip of the iceberg.'

'Are you suggesting we quit our jobs and jump in with you?'

'No, Samir. I am not.'

'Then get to the point, you don't need to give me this marketing spiel.'

'I have some statistics that I wanted to show you...'

'Not required, Jay, I believe you. I know what you have been up to, playing your old games in the art market. Tell me, what do you want?'

Jay knew from experience what 'I believe you' meant coming from Samir. It meant 'stop fucking wasting my time'. He was losing Samir's interest and needed to talk money fast. Okay, if that's how you want it, he thought.

'Samir, can you help me raise a $50-million alternate asset fund mandated to invest in art? Can it be done?'

Samir took one long sip of his beer. Jay waited for his reply.

'Obviously it can be done. But it's going to cost you. An alternate asset fund has never been done before.'

'What about the regulator?'

'Yeah, that could be a problem, given your record. Let me see, I will ask Pawan to get in touch with you. You know, that big guy from legal.'

'You mean that constipated bastard.'

'Yeah, him, he hasn't changed at all. Still keeps shitting

in his pants all the time.'

'And the fees?'

'Five per cent all inclusive.'

'Five? Are you serious?'

'Come on Jay, you don't think I know what's happening in the art market? If the picture were so rosy, you wouldn't be wasting your time here. Don't doubt my intelligence, it makes me very angry. You want me to do the heavy lifting and that is fine by me. But you will fucking pay for it.

'Now, let's shake hands and bottoms up.'

Jay walked away from the bar happy with the knowledge that the problems facing his gallery would be soon over. Very few investors in the financial sector understood the dynamics and aesthetics of the art market and consequently, they kept away from it. If an art fund could be created and managed by a professional gallery owner, like himself, then financial wealth could be channelized into the art market.

Two days later, he received a call from Pawan. There was excitement in his voice. 'There are some issues but it can be done.'

I am paying 5 per cent, obviously it can be done, Jay thought. He said, 'And what about the regulator?'

'Well, they still don't like you, but guess what? Their jurisdiction does not extend to alternate assets. You are one lucky bastard.'

'Okay, so what are the other issues?'

'Just to play it safe, we will market this fund to less than fifty investors so that it doesn't constitute an offer to the public according to the regulations. Samir has already reached out to a few private bankers who are excited to sell this product to their clients.'

'Aren't they always? Frankly, I don't care. These are operational matters; just get me my fifty bucks, Pawan.'

'We also need to resolve this issue regarding a conflict of interest between your roles as the manager of the fund on the one hand and as the owner of the gallery on the other.'

'Well, that shouldn't be a problem. Put a clause in the agreement stating that the fund will not directly purchase any painting from my gallery. I think that should solve it.'

'Yes, that should be fine. And one more thing, you had these beautiful marketing collaterals the other day that you were eager to show to Samir. Well, guess what? He has obliged you. Please send them to the office; we will use them in our story.'

'Bastards! You are all bastards,' Jay thought. He agreed to send them along.

Jay realised that nothing had changed over the past seven to eight years. These buggers could sell anything to anyone without even understanding what it was. The only thing that mattered was the fee they received.

'Ha!' he thought. 'These guys think that auctions are free from manipulation. Nothing is further from the truth.'

Jay doled out hefty sales commissions to raise the assets of the art fund. The bankers did a great job and accumulated over $40 million within a matter of a month. The who's who of corporate India made individual contributions ranging between $1 to 5 million. The fund was close-ended with a tenure of five years. Jay felt confident that this was long enough for him to create a stable and diverse market for the Navaratnas.

No sooner was the money received than Jay went on a hyper drive, buying paintings of the Navaratnas. He bought a few in the secondary market from some of his existing investors who had been pestering him for an exit. He thereafter bid for a few paintings at an auction. Unknown to the public, his own gallery was the anonymous seller of these paintings. These sales created the necessary liquidity at the gallery, which until now had been facing a major cash crunch.

Once the market had stabilised, he bought a few paintings by contemporaries. Over a short period of one year, he had deployed almost 50 per cent of the assets of the fund into the art market in India. This concentrated buying of the Navaratnas and a few contemporaries helped to improve the market sentiment while also raising the prices of their works. Consequently, in the year 2009-10, when most of the other funds were declaring losses, the art fund had returned a mammoth 50 per cent before fees to the investors.

≈

Chapter 24

Where Did These Come From?

Jay sat in his room with a pack of cigarettes and black coffee for company, his face beaming with self-confidence. His secretary, Maya, sat across the table, her face only slightly visible, hidden behind the thick pile of bills. Liquidity was tight, he had spent the previous week nudging clients to adhere to their promises and make payments, while simultaneously buying time from creditors.

It was early 2012 and despite the odds being against him, he had survived. The last four years had seen a severe recession in the art market, resulting in the closure of more galleries than had opened in the entire decade. Perhaps, even he would have met a similar fate, had it not been for the proceeds of the art fund which had helped to maintain stability and liquidity in the market of the Navaratnas.

The fund was fully invested now. In fact, in another year he had to find buyers to liquidate it. He had no clue how he was going to manage it. The art market was still sluggish. They hadn't sold a single painting last month. On the contrary, he was forced to buy one out of the dwindling cash reserves of the gallery to keep panic at bay. He had to find a solution, his financial resources were meagre and his clients were already invested up to their necks. He continuously toured the country organising exhibitions and meeting new investors; however, no matter how hard he worked, demand always struggled to absorb the ever increasing supply.

But then there was a silver lining amidst the clouds; the first signs of reversal in sentiment was faintly discernible.

'Sir, the landlord again called up yesterday,' Maya reminded him.

'What does he want?' he asked.

'The rent is outstanding for two months now,' she replied.

'Oh! Is it?'

He feigned ignorance in front of her but in truth he was aware of it. Just like he also knew that the state electricity board had threatened to disconnect supply if outstanding bills were not paid immediately. Further, two of his best employees had resigned the previous week due to non-payment of sales incentives, which were due for over six months.

But, he had no options, times were perilous and cash was king. He did what any successful businessman would have done in such a situation, make only those payments that were absolutely necessary, like the electricity bill, which he needed to pay immediately. The landlord was a good man, he had a large heart so he could pay him next month perhaps. But two of his best employees leaving the organisation worried him, this was a sentiment damper and needed to be arrested immediately.

'Maya, can't we stop them from leaving?' he asked. 'I am willing to pay 50 per cent of the incentive if they stay.'

She kept quiet. He could sense the inhibition in her mind.

'Don't worry,' he said. 'These are short-term tremors. I can see the light at the end of the tunnel. It is within our grasp, this is no time to give up.'

She nodded her head in agreement. She had complete confidence in his abilities she felt comforted by the calm and confidence on his face. He was a survivor. She had no reason to worry; she had an experienced captain who could steer the ship through any storm.

However, despite his optimism, there were tell-tale signs which highlighted the enormity of the situation. He was smoking far more than usual and if you looked carefully, you couldn't help but notice the twitching in his fingers. If only somehow he could maintain the status quo for a few more quarters, it would be smooth sailing all the way.

His thoughts were interrupted midway by the arrival of an invite to an upcoming auction.

As he examined the auction catalogue, glancing slowly through its pages, the expression on his face began to change. Long gone was the calmness and the optimism. With every passing page, his facial expressions became grimmer. By the time he had reached the end of the catalogue, he looked worried, desperate and a lot older.

This couldn't be true. From where did they come? he wondered.

There were no buyers and he knew there would be panic.

Suddenly, the sound of crashing cutlery brought his

thoughts back to the room. It was Maya; she was stunned and had dropped her cup of tea. For the first time, she saw anxiety and worry on her master's face. She didn't know what he knew. There were seven paintings of the Navaratnas listed in the auction catalogue for sale.

Seeing the look on her face, he asked her to leave immediately. After a moment's thought he got down to work. There was no time to waste.

He pulled out his records, his archives and notes. He wanted to find out more about these paintings. Whom did they belong to? Did they ever pass through his gallery?

After spending the better half of the afternoon, he realised that they hadn't. He couldn't find any records about them.

The next morning, he called up the auction house. They were tight-lipped, divulging only that the entire lot of seven came from two anonymous sellers. This was bad news, this could mean only one thing—even distinguished families who had remained patrons of the old masters were now selling their collection. If this was a reflection of things to come, then the market for the Navaratnas was doomed.

He tried to get some more information out of the auction house regarding the interest in the paintings. However, they gave him no further information. He panicked. 'Bastards! What do they have to lose? Only their commission. I, on the other hand, will lose it all, my shirt, my reputation, everything. In the past, I was happy even if I found a single new buyer every month. From where am I supposed to get the investors to buy seven paintings at one go?'

He called a meeting of his sales team. He sat with them

and ran through the client prospects and pipelines.

'Call them again,' he scowled. 'So what if they had refused earlier. Tell them, this is different, such quality of paintings haven't been seen in the market lately and these are the best of the lot. Tell them whatever is required but get a sale through.'

He led by example and made a few calls to the usual suspects himself—but he was turned down politely. In his desperation he made a few more calls, reaching out to even those investors whom he had neglected lately and was greeted with the choicest abuses.

Only a week remained for the auction and his position was no better. He felt no comfort that the paintings would be bought. Dejected, he sat alone in his office smoking, contemplating what to do next. Was this going to be the tidal wave he had been dreading all along, that would wipe his kingdom and drown his throne?

He heard the phone ring. It was Biswas. This was out of the blue. He hadn't heard from him in months. 'What does he want? I am in no mood for a polite conversation.' After a moment's hesitation, he picked the phone.

'How are you, old chap?' asked Jay. 'Haven't heard from you in ages.'

'Very well, Jay, and you?' replied Biswas.

'In the first instance, I didn't want to involve you in my business problems, Biswas, but since you ask, I am in some serious trouble. Do you think you can you help me?' said Jay.

'I can help only if I know what happened,' replied Biswas.

Jay narrated the entire sob story to him. There was silence.

For a moment he thought that the line had been disconnected.

'Biswas, are you still there?' he asked.

'Yes, yes, I am very much here, Jay.'

Then again there was a moment of silence.

'Are you telling me that you don't have a single investor to buy these paintings?' asked Biswas.

There was both disbelief and concern in his voice.

'Yes, that is exactly what I am telling you, Biswas,' replied Jay. 'I don't have a single investor to buy these paintings. Not at the moment at least. I mean, there is still a week to go but it will be a miracle if I manage something.'

'Okay,' replied Biswas. 'Let me see what I can do.'

And the line went dead.

Jay looked at the phone receiver in his hand, not sure what to make of his conversation. He had a simple understanding with Biswas which had worked well for them over the past ten years. He managed the business whereas Biswas worked on research and academia. Biswas didn't wish to be involved in commercial matters and it was just fine with Jay. This was the reason he had not thought it fit to call him for help.

But now he was intrigued. Biswas said that he was going to help. There was a glimmer of hope, a speck of light in an otherwise dark tunnel. He hung on to it and waited anxiously for Biswas to revert.

As luck would have it, he didn't have to wait too long. Biswas called back later in the night.

'Go and meet this museum curator in Delhi tomorrow,' he said. 'I have fixed a meeting for you with the curator at eleven in the morning.'

Jay was thrilled and asked him if they had shown any interest.

'I don't know how these things work, Jay, but they got a grant from the government only last month and are flush with funds,' he replied. 'The ball is now in your court. I can't do anymore.'

Jay thanked Biswas profusely.

The next day he was in Delhi, sipping on a cup of tea with the curator of the museum. The meeting started rather casually and he was a little disappointed with the reception. He didn't see any sense of urgency in the body language of the curator. The auction was in six days, so he wondered if the curator had agreed to meet him out of compulsion. After all, very few people could have refused Biswas, who was a larger-than-life figure in the world of art history and academia.

However, as one cup of tea led to another, followed by a lunch invitation, things began to get interesting. Jay had a sixth sense for these things—he could decipher the subtle clues which most people would miss, the change in body language, the style and scope of questions. He could tell when it was merely curiosity and when it was much more. And he liked how this discussion was progressing. After five long hours, he was finally shaking hands with the curator. He had convinced them to bid for four paintings at the auction. The museum had some issues regarding his engagement; they couldn't be officially seen bidding under his advice. But those were matters of detail, which could be sorted out another day. For now, he was relieved, the only thing that mattered was that he had a committed bidder for four of the paintings.

He flew back to Mumbai thanking his lucky stars and Biswas, without whom this would not have been possible. Five days still remained for the auction and he got down to work as soon as he landed in Mumbai, taking a feedback from his sales team who were continuously on the job day and night, trying to locate new investors while deepening their relationship with existing ones. There was one lead, an inbound call by one Mr Deepak Patel, who had requested for a meeting the day after.

'Hang on, you mean Deepak Patel as in "The Deepak Patel", the business tycoon whose rags-to-riches story is the stuff legends are made of?'

There was silence on the other side of the call—obviously they didn't know.

'How many times I have told you guys to identify the caller? Anyway, he must have given a contact number; call up and find out more and get back to me.'

He was elated. Deepak Patel was a potential gold mine with unlimited wealth. He had made a few purchases of lesser known contemporaries in the past but was not known to be a serious collector. Hence this call from his office intrigued him.

Patel was unpopular in the art fraternity and was spoken about with much disdain. The old-timers called him names, saying he was a loud, flashy, moneyed man with little taste. But Jay didn't care; in his line of work, he didn't have the luxury of being choosy. Any investor would do, so long as he paid in cash.

The next day, he heard back from his office that the investor was indeed Deepak Patel, the business tycoon. Jay spent the day preparing for his meeting. If he could somehow convince Patel to bid for the remaining three paintings at the auction, he would be home.

He arrived at Patel's office at Nariman Point at nine sharp. Patel exceeded his wildest expectations. Despite all he had heard about him being loud and flashy, nothing could have prepared him for the gaudy room that shimmered in gold. Patel himself appeared to be a little overdressed. He couldn't pinpoint what was wrong with his attire, the suit fit well and was undoubtedly of the finest fabric, but something seemed to be out of place.

He immediately proceeded to the task at hand, that of convincing Patel to bid for the three remaining paintings at the auction. However, despite his sweet talk and sales spiel, Patel was not swayed and remained focused on his own agenda. He told Jay that he was interested in only one of the paintings, the portrait of a veiled woman by Rabindranath Tagore.

'Jay, I want you to be personally present at the auction and bid for me.'

'But Mr Patel, I would much rather bid discreetly over the phone. Otherwise I risk driving the prices higher.'

'Please explain yourself?'

'Well, sir, I am extremely well known in the art circles and my aggressive bidding can easily sway the sentiment in the auction room, inviting competing bids and driving up the prices.'

'Oh! I see, so you are that well known, are you? That's even better. You see, I need that painting at all costs, price is not a consideration and I intend on making a big splash when I buy it.'

'Your celebrity status in the art circles works to my benefit. Once you have won the final bid, please do be kind enough to identify me in front of the entire art fraternity as the winner of the painting.'

'You will obviously get me a seat in the front row at the auction.'

'Obviously I will,' Mr Patel.

As he left the meeting, he was amazed—what a crazy man, he thought to himself. This wasn't about money; there was something far deeper at play here, perhaps ego and much more. Even after a decade, the art market still managed to throw an unexpected googly at him every now and then.

He called up the auction house as he stepped out of the elevator.

'Please reserve a seat in the front row for Mr Deepak Patel.'

'It will be done, Mr Malhotra.'

'Also send me a few passes; I need a few of my clients to attend.'

'Would five suffice, sir?'

'No, make that ten.'

Now that he had the auction reasonably covered, he wanted to invite some of his jittery clients. He hoped that their nerves would be calmed by the results of the auction.

≈

Chapter 25

The Neglected Investor

It was well past midnight. One of India's major steel plants was the site of much hustle bustle, with thousands of workers slogging at the shops. Under the glare of the spot lights one could see the massive blast furnaces melting raw iron ore into molten iron. Everything about this steel plant was larger than life, reflecting the ambitions of its owner who was known to dream big.

Deepak Patel had exhibited entrepreneurial flair and a risk-taking appetite from an early age. His lack of fluency in the English language had forced him to drop his college education. He had started his first business venture of selling paan leaves in Mumbai in his teens. On a visit to Mumbai with his uncle, Deepak had asked the shop owner they had purchased paan from if he could supply him with a popular variant of the leaves from Kolkata. Cornered by this enquiry from the nephew of a good customer, the shop owner had obliged and consequently introduced him to a few other paan vendors in Mumbai.

A week after this interaction, Deepak had caught a train from Kolkata bound for Mumbai, armed with a bunch of paan leaves. Travelling in the unreserved general compartment, he had sat next to the door adjacent to the toilet until his arrival in Mumbai two days later. During this period, he had constantly sprinkled water on the paan leaves to ensure that they remained green and did not dry in the heat of the Indian summer. After supplying paan leaves to the vendors in Mumbai, he purchased toys which were much in demand in Kolkata and caught a train for the return journey. He made several of these trips every month for most of his college years, with each trip netting him a few hundred rupees. By the time his friends had passed out of college with degrees, Deepak had successfully saved a small quantum of risk capital.

This risk capital was not sufficient to establish a manufacturing entity. That required a much larger capital commitment for plant and machinery but it was significant for a trading business, where investments were required only in working capital. However, the trading business did not result in significant profits. For that matter, no business could have generated extraordinary profits in an efficient market. Extraordinary profit was possible only in a monopolistic environment, where existing rules and regulations could be bent or from enjoying advantages which were not available to others. Deepak was a fair person, willing to share his earnings with those who helped facilitate and grow his business.

The city of Bhilai in central India had emerged as a bustling centre of trade and commerce, making many merchants like him millionaires overnight. The fact that it housed the largest public sector iron and steel plant in the country obviously had something to do with it. Accordingly, Deepak began a business that traded in coal and scrap metal in Bhilai. By supplying lower grade coal with impurities and higher ash content and raising invoices for the more expensive coking coal required in the steel-making process, he managed to earn exorbitant profits within a short period of time. These profits were thereafter deployed to buy quality metal scrap at throwaway prices, which was then sold to private merchants and steel producers in the region for handsome profits. Obviously, this business was below the table and was successful only with the active collaboration and connivance of employees of the public sector undertaking, who were active partners in his business. The going was so good that within a few years he had accumulated sufficient capital to start dreaming of establishing an industrial undertaking. What could be better than an iron and steel company, since he already had access to cheap raw material?

But establishing an industrial undertaking was a different ball game in terms of scale and complexity. No one in their right minds established it with their own capital; it was far too risky. The tried and tested model was to seek the financial support of the public sector banks. While you could wonder at the saying that behind every successful man there was a woman, there was no questioning the fact that behind every successful industrialist there was a public sector bank chairman. But Deepak didn't know any. However, he didn't allow this problem to become an impediment to his plans.

True to his entrepreneurial spirit, he made a few visits to Delhi and Mumbai in search of intermediaries and power brokers and was soon dining and entertaining the chairmen of several banks.

Within a few months, his proposal with inflated project costs was approved. Funds were siphoned off by inflating the cost of equipment and material and subsequently re-deployed into the project as enhanced equity capital of the promoters. Realising that his largest cost after iron ore was power, he openly resorted to stealing power from the state electricity distribution company. Rumour had it that he would stand in front of his factory with a briefcase full of cash, waiting for the inspectors of the state electricity board to raid his establishment. Whenever the raids did happen, they were never allowed to enter the establishment and instead ended at a refreshment shop adjacent to the factory gate, where commerce was discussed and money was exchanged over cups of hot tea and Parle biscuits. With his cost of production being almost 10 per cent cheaper than any other steel producer in the country, Deepak's steel empire grew by leaps and bounds in size and across geographical spaces.

As he sat in his penthouse at the top floor of Maker Chambers at Nariman Point, Mumbai, admiring the lights from the Queens' Necklace on Marine Drive below, he pondered his past. Dressed in a $50,000 suit, specifically fitted and tailored by Brioni, London, with the rarest French and British fabric money could buy, wearing a Patek Philippe on his left wrist, Hermes tie and cufflinks and Louis Vuitton shoes, one would not be wrong in concluding that Deepak was perhaps overdressed, the fine clothing a contrast to his retro look of sporting a moustache and oily hair with a side parting. It was almost as if he were trying too hard, the clothes compensating for his humble beginnings, lack of college education or fluency in English.

Similarly, the Italian marble on the floor paled in comparison to the walls and the ceilings of the room, all of which shimmered in gold. Gold was the theme in the office and covered everything present, from the leather desk and chairs to the fountain pen on the desk to the frames of some of the paintings that adorned the walls. The interiors had been done by a leading interior decorator who had created a similar setting for a fashion diva. However, the end product was too subtle for Mr Patel's liking and had to be subsequently re-done in a tone of gold that was garish in its appearance, thereby making a subtle room into a gaudy reflection.

Today, on his fifty-fifth birthday, Deepak Patel was recognised as one of the most successful first-generation entrepreneurs in the country with a business empire that stretched across steel, infrastructure and construction. While these successful business ventures had created substantial financial wealth and economic capital, what he really longed for was capital of a social and cultural kind.

He had utilised his companies to seek corporate membership of the most exclusive clubs in India, namely the Cricket Club in Mumbai and the Delhi Gymkhana Club, where the waiting period for private memberships was longer than thirty-five years. He had trained in the necessary social etiquette for over a fortnight to attend the 'At Home' function at the Delhi Gymkhana Club, held by the committee to meet people invited to become prospective members of the club. He enjoyed his membership of these exclusive clubs and utilised them on every possible occasion to entertain his guests.

Likewise, in return for corporate sponsorship for the Institute of Management in the newly established university in Chhattisgarh, he had been honoured with a doctorate in the field of Family Business and Entrepreneurship.

Fine art had enjoyed the patronage of kings and the social elite for many generations and its ownership was almost universally associated with high culture and taste. It might just be the window of opportunity that he had been waiting for, something that would guarantee him access to the final frontier of the elite in Delhi and Mumbai. It was with this in mind that he had approached Jay Malhotra to bid on his behalf to buy the artwork of Rabindranath Tagore at the auction. He had instructed Jay that so long as he sat in his chair at the auction, Jay should continue bidding for the masterpiece; the price was not relevant. Deepak wished to make a splash before the exclusive art circles of Delhi and Mumbai. He wanted to be publicly identified in front of the entire art fraternity as the owner of the painting.

Thus, while he did not have the family background that would have allowed him to inherit the status of the rich and famous, he had successfully institutionalised and objectified cultural capital by obtaining educational recognition and artwork associated with them.

≋

Chapter 26

Forgeries Rule the Roost

Authenticating artwork had become a risky business the world over. With millions of dollars riding on the outcome of the process, experts who differed with the opinions held by collectors and investors often faced legal hassles.

Money, higher returns and greed was creating friction and lawsuits in the art industry. In the earlier days, expert opinions regarding art used to be mere opinions rather than leverage in legal battles. Some level of risk was tolerable, with experts willing to put their reputations on the line for a remarkable, undocumented work of art. Similarly, they had little fear in letting someone know, nicely, that the work in their possession was not an original work by a widely recognised artist but a forgery. The stakes were much lower and a lawsuit was a rarity. However, those days were long over, a sweet distant memory of the past. Too much money and big egos were at stake now. Where art was once more an object of admiration than self-glorification, high-stakes collecting had become a blood sport.

With so much money and time being wasted on these legal matters, a few well-known art foundations like those of Warhol and Pollock had stopped authentication altogether. Most experts today kept their professional opinion to themselves regarding the authenticity of paintings. The art of authentication was not standardised and involved a certain amount of subjectivity, especially where provenance was difficult to establish. Evidence or the lack thereof could be given varying importance, resulting in different outcomes. As a result, it was possible that the opinion of experts often differed with respect to some artworks.

At a recently held auction in India, the authenticity of a number of paintings by renowned artists like Tagore, Raza and Husain was disputed. Despite this opposition, the auction went ahead, facilitated by lawyers who issued notices to everyone who had doubted the authenticity of the works. The auction house had in-house experts who had vouched for the authenticity of the pieces sold. In a particular case, a painting had been authenticated by both a senior art historian and a critic only to be disputed by the artist's son as a forgery. Issues regarding authenticity had also arisen at a few auctions earlier. Generally, in such cases, the norm was that the auction house would remove the questionable painting from the auction process. However, this auction was unique; it was perhaps the first time that an auction house had used the legal route in India. Lawyers had finally arrived at the lavish Indian art banquet.

The art industry in India had its own peculiar problems. Its infrastructure was not very well developed, curatorial practices and historical study being almost non-existent. There was a dearth of financial benchmarking, publications, archiving, exhibitions and such supports that build the credibility of art. Most of those who had entered the art industry did so to make a quick buck irrespective of methods, due diligence and wider consequences, unwilling to accept infrastructure building as their responsibility. Taking advantage of greedy aspiring culture, galleries had mushroomed all over the country. Framing shops called themselves art galleries and art gallery owners called themselves historians. Affluent housewives with the right rhetoric but non-existent knowledge sold art through Page 3-type wine and cheese art openings. The art gallery had become the new alternative hub for socialite evenings. People without experience, expertise, reading or aesthetic exposure became art dealers.

There were very few institutions which actively catalogued and documented works of the masters. There was a great need for proper documentation, regulation and transparency. Several Indian artists, especially those who had worked in the early decades of the twentieth century and whose paintings now commanded millions did not maintain records of paintings they created or the people they sold it to. The early works of these artists changed hands for a few hundred rupees. There was little to prove that these works that were now coming up for sale were genuine.

Fakes were always associated with the art industry in India but until two decades back they had never found their way into the mainstream market. In 1990, an art gallery based in south India sold some work supposedly belonging to Husain whose authenticity was contested by the artist's son who raised an alarm after he spotted a forgery from the popular Raja and Rani series.

In 2011, at the 150th birth anniversary of Rabindranath Tagore, an exhibition of the artists' works was held at the prestigious Government College of Arts and Crafts in Kolkata. After some art connoisseurs and collectors raised objections regarding the authenticity of a few works of art on display, an enquiry was held by the Archaeological Survey of India under instructions from the Government of India. It was discovered that more than 75 per cent of the works on display were forgeries. The problem of forgeries in the contemporaries was accentuated by the fact that a large number of the forgeries were promoted by family members of the artists themselves. Due to a dispute within the artist's family after his death or, in some cases, even while he was alive, different family members were actively involved in faking the artworks of the artist to make quick money. In 2008, when a gallery in New Delhi presented an exclusive solo show of Somnath Hore, the artist's daughter herself came forward to say that the works in the show were forgeries. In this specific case, the gallery in question had been misled and taken for a ride by one of the relatives of the late artist.

In 2009, another well-known gallery in Delhi got into trouble by displaying works that supposedly belonged to Raza, who interestingly, was present during the opening of the show. The gallery had to scrap the show as the artist himself identified almost all the works as forgeries. Interestingly, once again all these works came from one the artist's relatives. There were also recorded instances where the artwork had been authenticated by the issue of a certificate of authentication by one member of the family, only to be called a forgery later.

Some artists were known to seek active assistance from their students and disciples in the creation of artwork, only to sign them with their own names later. These students and disciples had since been engaged by the underground forgery market to flood the art industry with quality fakes created in the same style as the artist. They were very difficult to differentiate from the original work, even for the tested eyes of the experts.

To add to the complexity, many artists in India were known to sell their own artworks in cash without any receipt of sale. This was sometimes done at the request of the buyer who didn't want to purchase via a cheque and preferred using his undisclosed income to make these investments. It also helped the artist as he did not have to pay tax on these unrecognised sales. For every piece they sold via a cheque with the corresponding receipt, they sold two in cash without any trail or record. In fact, the sales in cash were often done at a slight discount and were sometimes not even signed by the artist. These pieces were not fakes, since they were created by the artists themselves. However, due to the lack of a trail, it was difficult to prove their provenance, especially after the death of the artist.

With over 5000 students graduating from art schools in the country and only a few succeeding as artists, they provided ready fodder for the art forgery market. Sometimes, these students were engaged by the galleries themselves to create quality fakes that were then sold to unsuspecting investors as works of the masters.

≈

Chapter 27

Who is Provenance?

It was the most high-profile Diwali party of the year. It was being held at a farmhouse in the suburbs of Delhi. In attendance were the who's who of corporate India, senior government officials (including some politicians) and the entire art fraternity. The driveway and porch were filled with custom-built Bentleys, Rolls-Royces, Maybachs, the odd Lamborghini and Hindustan Ambassadors which, till date, continued to be the vehicle of choice for the mighty in the power corridors of Delhi.

The party was meant to be a launch pad for Deepak Patel to announce his grand entrance into the exclusive art industry. Only a month ago, he had successfully acquired the *Portrait of a Woman*, a masterpiece by Rabindranath Tagore. The painting now adorned the walls of his living room. He still remembered basking in glory as he went on stage to accept the painting overlooked by the art fraternity.

He called out for his secretary. 'Jaya, show me that speech

once more. I want to take a quick glance.'

'Here you go, Mr Patel.'

Jaya wondered why he was so nervous. This was the third time he had read that piece of paper containing details of the painting.

'Jaya, I plan to give this speech standing in front of my latest acquisition.

She adjusted his tie knot, which was a little out of place.

'These bastards have excluded me for far too long. Who can argue that I am successful? I have reached the zenith of the corporate world, established one of the most revered groups in India. And I have done so by beating the shit out of many of these third-generation industrialists who are part of the art fraternity.'

She nodded her head in agreement.

'However, despite my wealth and riches, I am apparently not successful enough to be a member of this exclusive group. Who the hell are these people to hold me back? What qualifications do they possess that I don't have?

'Tonight is going to be my night; I will finally rub their noses in the dirt. This will be a new beginning for me.'

The art fraternity detested people like Patel, the nouveau riche, first-generation entrepreneurs who had created successful business empires and accumulated substantial wealth. They were generally held to be rustic and crude. Despite their wealth, they lacked exquisite taste and cultural intellect, prerequisites to be accepted in the exclusive art circles. After all, the art circles were the guardians of high culture and taste.

However, with the evolution of the art world into an

industry, the art fraternity couldn't have survived without the money and wealth of people like Patel. Patel's wealth was essential in driving the demand and prices of contemporaries and old masters to astronomical heights. Hence, despite their extreme disgust for this new breed of investors, the art fraternity had no option but to accept them into their exclusive guild.

The *Portrait of a Woman* was displayed in the main hall of the living room, surrounded by works of some lesser known contemporary artists. After receiving his guests and exchanging pleasantries, Patel asked his staff to make an announcement asking all guests to move into the living room.

As people started assembling in the main hall admiring the masterpiece, Patel quickly took out the small piece of paper containing his speech. Due to his nervousness, despite reading it thrice already he had forgotten every word written of it. As he was about to begin his speech, he heard a rather loud, animated discussion taking place among a group of people in the hall.

He looked towards Jaya who was standing next to him. 'Who are these people creating the ruckus? I don't recognise any of them.'

'Sir, I don't know, but I guess they must be from the art fraternity,' she replied.

'Yeah, but this is supposed to be my party. Who the fuck is taking my place as the centre of attention?'

As he moved towards the centre of the huddle, he heard the word 'provenance' being used liberally.

He took a step back. 'Provenance, what provenance? There is nothing about provenance in this speech.'

He whispered into Jaya's ears, 'Who is provenance?'

Patty, wearing a crimson red sari, was standing in the middle of the huddle and speaking aloud.

'I had an opportunity to examine this painting before the auction. It has an incomplete provenance—there is a gap in the known ownership of the artwork from the time it was created by Tagore to its first recorded sale. I asked the auction house how they could be certain of its pedigree. They informed me that they had an expert opinion. However, I wasn't comfortable and advised my clients not to bid for it.'

Then looking straight into the eyes of Patel, who now stood dumbfounded in front of her, she said, 'Mr Patel, I wonder who was advising you. For all you know, you might have bought a fake for top dollars.'

There was a furore in the room. An insider of the art fraternity, and the owner of distinguished galleries, was raising serious allegations about the provenance of a painting. That was not to be taken lightly. Patty had raised doubts about the authenticity of the masterpiece. As of that moment, it had become worthless.

By the time Patel realised what had transpired, it was all over. He could hear loud giggles and see smirks as people spoke to each other. It was ironic; the party which was meant to be his launching pad had become his grave. He had been reduced to a laughing stock. The members of the art fraternity were in splits, laughing wildly at Patel who had bought a forgery. And worse, he had done it by exceeding the reserve price.

He looked at the speech in his hand. It was irrelevant now as no one cared for the painting anymore. He crumpled the piece of paper in sheer anger and left the premises. The party ended even before the appetisers could be served.

Patty walked away from the party smiling. She was enjoying the renewed attention she was getting from the art fraternity lately. The insiders could feel the tide turning and had already started aligning themselves to her. It was only a matter of time before she re-established herself as the queen of the art market.

'Give me a little time and I will have this Patel dancing to my tunes,' she said to herself. 'He will also be Jay Malhotra's biggest nightmare, if I can help it.'

≈

Chapter 28

All Hell Breaks Loose!

It was the day after Diwali. Jay had reached the gallery early in the morning. He asked the security guard to open his office while he moved towards the espresso machine in the kitchen to make himself a double shot. This coffee machine was the best investment he had made in years. He intended to get some work done and clean his inbox before the staff began to arrive.

Every day was becoming more difficult for him. The stars were no longer shining on him. Despite all odds, he lingered on, sometimes even surprising himself. However, he still had no idea how he was going to survive the rest of the year. A little over a month had elapsed since the auction in Mumbai, the results of which had been better than his wildest expectations. As a result, he had managed some breathing space, reorganising his efforts towards finding new clients for the Navaratnas. He had succeeded in finding a few leads, but the numbers were just not enough to absorb the sellers in the market.

He heard the vibrating noise of the mobile phone. He looked at his watch. It was only nine in the morning who could be calling him at this hour? The name flashing on the display panel read Vicky Arora. 'What the fuck does he want this early in the morning? Did I sell him anything lately?' Jay pondered this for a little while and then answered the call.

'Hello, Vicky. How are you buddy? You're up early today; was it a dry day in Delhi yesterday? Is everything all right?'

'Haven't you heard the rumours, Jay?'

'No. What rumours?'

'I got a call from my cousin Nikki late last night. You know, the same guy who is a defence dealer.'

'Yeah, yeah, go ahead.'

'Well, he was at a party thrown by your client the day before yesterday.'

'Which client?'

'That Patel fellow you bought that Tagore for.'

'Okay…'

'Apparently, the painting is a fake.'

'What? Who said it's a fake? Don't fuck with me early in the morning, Vicky!'

'No, boss, I am serious. There was this woman at the party who raised some serious shit regarding the provenance of the painting.'

'Questionable provenance does not mean that the painting is a fake.'

'I don't know all that. I thought I should call you up brother; I am a well-wisher after all.'

He received half a dozen calls over the next two hours

from supposed well-wishers. He knew that all of them were gossip-mongers having a field day at his expense. As he pieced together the happenings at the party, he realised that it was none other than Patty who had raised the issue of provenance in front of the entire art community to humiliate Patel.

She is back, the back-stabbing bitch, he thought to himself. This was the first time that she had attacked him when he wasn't present to defend himself. He was surprised by her actions, despite the fact that she had made no bones in the past that she vehemently disliked him.

'It's been over a decade since we parted ways,' he thought, 'and our separation was not the most amicable. However, we both had our own selfish reasons: she used me as her arm candy, showcasing me wherever she went, while I played along only to learn the dynamics of the art business.

'I am aware the she was very upset with me and had vowed to take revenge when the time was right and I was at my most vulnerable.

'Even though she is beyond her prime, she still wields a lot of influence in the art industry. She still has her coterie of art enthusiasts and connoisseurs who raise issues in line with her overall direction. It's understandable that once she raised concerns about the provenance of the painting, the same were reverberated by others in the art circle.

'I must be careful about how I approach this matter. It doesn't matter whether the concerns regarding the provenance of the painting are genuine or were raised only to show me in a bad light in front of my client and the art fraternity in general.

'You have made a smart move, Patty; I wasn't present to

defend myself. However, I wonder why you attacked now. Was this based on an inference that my position in the market is weakening? Can the art insiders see that I am weak, my hands are overstretched; and perhaps this is the best time to hit back at me and seek revenge?

'These rumours about the authenticity of the painting are neither good for my reputation nor for the market of the Navaratnas that I have created so painstakingly. I must quell them immediately. With such issues being raised, the value of the painting has been decimated. I must immediately take action to protect my reputation and meet with Deepak Patel. The poor bastard must be in a lot of pain.'

When Jay reached the office the next morning, he found Patel looking rather calm and composed. Slowly, Patel narrated the entire incident to him in detail.

'Jay, the Diwali party was meant to be my launching pad into the exclusive art circles. I made all the arrangements, paid attention to the finest details, invited the right mix of people. It's funny but I had even prepared a bloody speech for the occasion. Instead, the party ended even before it started and I was reduced to a joke. I can still hear the smirks in my head, people speaking in soft undertones that money and wealth cannot buy taste and cultural capital, which takes generations to cultivate. This was a cruel joke played on me.'

There was silence in the room; Jay could see the rising anger in Patel's eyes, his face turning red. All the calm was dissipating.

Then suddenly he roared, 'Why didn't you attend the party, Jay Malhotra? Why were you not present to defend me? Did you have an inkling that this was going to happen? You left me like a sheep amongst the wolves. Get to the bottom of this; I am not pointing my fingers at you just yet. Hold all possible enquiries and revert to me. If I feel that I have been cheated, then I will not leave any stone upturned to exact revenge.'

Patel was now trembling with anger.

'If I don't handle this matter delicately then Patel will be mine and the art industry's biggest nightmare. He will fight a very public and vocal battle and in doing so, bring the entire art industry into disrepute,' Jay thought. He gathered himself and spoke.

'Mr Patel, sir, I can help you only if you trust me. There was no hidden agenda behind my not attending the party. In retrospect, perhaps I should have and I apologise for the same. Please calm down. Don't worry, all is not lost. They have only doubted the provenance; this does not prove that the painting is a forgery. I will reach out to an expert of eminence. My dear friend Biswas Mukherjee is an authority on Rabindranath Tagore. I will request him to carry out an authentication for the painting to arrive at the truth. Please give me till tomorrow evening to revert to you.'

As he walked out of the office, Jay wondered why Patel was so upset with him. He had merely been bidding on his behalf at the auction. This wasn't about the painting or money.

'This entire incident has left a deep mark on Patel's ego. Now he wants his pound of flesh and if I do not act fast then the first casualty is likely to be me,' he realised.

I must reach out to Biswas immediately and request him to help me out.

Chapter 29

No One Wants to Know

Biswas was enjoying the winter sun on his terrace garden and sipping a mug of black coffee. He was reading an article on the life of Wolfgang Beltracchi, one of the greatest art forgers of all time, responsible for perhaps the biggest art forgery scandal of the post-war era in terms of both the scope and perfection of the paintings and how well they had been marketed.

Biswas' work required that he keep himself updated on the latest happenings in the world of art forgery and authentication. Beltracchi was only recently discovered by the art world after he became infamous by revealing his true identity as a forger and surrendering in a negotiated deal with the German courts. This was surprising, as he had been active for over two decades, a time period during which he is rumoured to have created forgeries of works by Max Ernst, Fernand Léger, Heinrich Campendonk, André Derain, Max Pechstein, classic modernist paintings, most of them by French and German expressionists and many others. No one knows for certain the extent of these works currently afloat in the art market.

Biswas smiled as he read the last sentence and wondered if it should have read 'no one wanted to know' rather than 'no one knew'.

Beltracchi had exposed a system where there were no pre-defined parameters which defined the value of a painting, a system that made erratic decisions about which piece was worth a lot of money and which was worth nothing at all. He made millions by creating hundreds of forgeries and fooling everyone. Christie's had featured a Beltracchi fake on a catalogue cover. The Metropolitan Museum of Art in New York was among a host of famous galleries that had fallen prey to his talent.

Biswas shook his head in disgust. 'Nothing has changed over the past few decades', he thought. 'We were suckers then and we continue to remain suckers today.' He wondered how many more Beltracchis were out there who hadn't yet been discovered by the art fraternity.

As he reached out for another mug of coffee, he heard his phone ringing.

'Good afternoon, Jay! How are you?'

'Biswas, I need to meet you urgently. Where are you right now?'

'I am at home. Are you coming over? Is everything okay?'

'Let's discuss it when I get there.'

Biswas reflected that Jay had been getting into a lot of trouble lately. 'Only last month I helped him at the auction.

I wonder what it is now. I hope he isn't expecting anymore clients from me. I don't have any and even if I did, I won't help him. This was not part of our deal.'

He turned back to the article but was no longer as relaxed as before, looking every now and then at the stairs leading to the terrace, waiting for Jay to arrive.

Just then, he heard the sound of someone coming up the stairs in haste.

Presuming that the person climbing the stairs was Jay, he said, 'You have a long life, boy. I was thinking about you, wondering what mess you have gotten yourself into now.' There was an element of sarcasm in his voice.

Jay appeared on the terrace, looking rather tired and worn down.

'You look like shit. Haven't been sleeping lately, have you?'

'Thanks, you noticed. I look like this because I am in deep shit, Biswas.'

'What happened?'

'At the auction last month, I bid for a Tagore for one of my clients, Deepak Patel. This guy is a big fish, has a big ego. It turns out that there are gaps in the provenance of the painting I bid for.'

'So what? Tell Mr Patel that very few paintings have complete provenance.'

'Thanks, I tried that. But there is more to the story. Apparently, Patty got frisky with this guy and told him that the thing might be a fake. And now he thinks that I fucked up. Even worse, he thinks that I might have deliberately fingered him.'

'Oh, I see. Now that is a problem. Patty is really good at this kind of thing. So what do you want from me?'

'Please authenticate this painting. You need to save my ass.'

'I will accept this project but everyone knows that we both go a long way back. People will cry conflict of interest, fingers will be raised regarding the objectivity of the authentication process. Hence, I will create a collegium and ask them to carry out the authentication. They will obviously work under my guidance.'

'Do whatever you want, Biswas. Just give me the result I want. This painting needs to be authentic, otherwise I will be doomed.'

Biswas's indulgent tone disappeared. 'Boy, I will carry out the authentication exercise but be assured that your desires will not influence the results in any manner. If the painting is a forgery then so be it. How dare you question my integrity? How dare you?'

'Oh shit, I shouldn't have said that,' Jay thought. He realised he had made a big mistake.

'Leave my house.'

'I am sorry, Biswas. I didn't mean to…'

'Get out now!'

Despite the nudge from Biswas, as he left the house, he shouted back, 'I will send the painting in a few days!' In retrospect, he wondered if he had done the right thing in giving the assignment to Biswas. He had been foolish to think that Biswas would change his ways to help him out. He should have known better than to question Biswas's integrity. But he didn't have any option; these were pressing times and he was in deep shit.

Jay called Patel and informed him that after much persuasion, Biswas had agreed to lead a collegium of experts to authenticate the painting.

To save face, Patel immediately gave an interview to media.

'I am very pained by the events of the past week. Questions have been raised regarding the provenance of the painting in my possession. I have put the auction house on notice; they are cooperating with us to get to the bottom of this issue. I am happy to inform you that I have independently engaged the services of a leading expert to give his opinion on this matter.'

≋

Chapter 30

The Mystery of the Veiled Woman

Biswas sat in his office, still furious over his discussion with Jay the previous day. He kept going over the same words in his mind time and again. Every time he did so, he got even more upset.

The morning papers didn't bring any respite. On the contrary, they stressed him further. There was a long article on the third page: 'Mr Biswas Mukherjee, the author of the Catalogue Raisonné on Rabindranath Tagore, has agreed to form a collegium to undertake the authentication of the painting.' Journalists had been calling his office since morning, trying to get a byte from him for their stories. He preferred working in isolation and despised these high-profile cases. He knew that from now on, every action of his would be under media scrutiny.

The painting in question had been sourced from a renowned auction house. These auction houses had elaborate processes for determining the provenance and were backed by in-house experts whose opinion was always taken before putting any painting up for sale. In fact, the auction house under scrutiny had sought Biswas' opinion on a few other paintings on sale that night. However, despite these comprehensive processes, they were known to make mistakes at times. In May 2000, after both Christie's and Sotheby's had finalised their auction catalogue, they realised that they were both offering Paul Gauguin's 1885 *Vase de Fleurs*. Both the artworks were sent to an expert and it was found that the one displayed in Christie's catalogue, gently put, was not right.

Biswas asked one of his assistants to get in touch with the auction house and get all possible information in their possession on the provenance of the painting. He didn't want to re-invent the wheel; the data provided by the auction house would be a good starting point.

He had already reached out to a few of his friends and ex-colleagues who were renowned experts on the Bengal School and on Rabindranath Tagore. This collective approach would ensure that individual biases did not impact the final outcome. He hoped that the finding of the collegium would put to rest the speculation and rumour-mongering in the art fraternity and restore the value of the artwork.

Over the next few days, all the members of the collegium arrived in Mumbai to commence work. Biswas held a closed-door meeting in which they discussed the broad parameters and strategy they would use to carry out the authentication exercise. It was decided that since Biswas was the author of the Catalogue Raisonné on Tagore, he wouldn't be directly involved in the authentication exercise. His views and opinions would be sought by the collegium as and when required. This would help in the formation of a balanced and fair opinion which could then be communicated to Biswas, who as chairman of the collegium would take the final decision. Once the meeting was over, they were provided all the information that had been sourced from the auction house, together with the original painting, which had only arrived the previous evening.

The jivanadevata, the lady behind the veil, has been one of the most important themes in Tagore's works and has found ample representation in the corpus of his works, including poems, songs, writings and paintings. However, the identification of the woman behind the veil has always remained shrouded in mystery.

She is the boat woman without the veil in the song, *'Tumi epar opar karo'* (1905) and the woman he meets on the dark shoreline in the song, *'Ratri eshe jethay'* (1910). One of the most detailed descriptions is in the poem titled, 'Sindhu Pare' (1896) in which he instantly recognises her as his jivanadevata as she reveals herself by lifting her veil at the wedding.

Tagore had once mentioned to Nandalal Bose that he was deeply impacted by the untimely death of his sister-in-law, Kadambari Devi, and she continued to inspire his work. Tagore continued to create endless variations of portraits of a woman with a pensive face and large, unwavering soulful eyes.

In 1917, Tagore wrote to Amiya Chakravarty who was sixteen years old and would later become his literary secretary: 'Once, when I was about your age, I suffered a devastating sorrow, similar to yours now. A very close relative of mine committed suicide, and she had been my life's total support, right from childhood. And so with her unexpected death it was as if the earth itself receded from beneath my feet, as though the skies above me all went dark. My universe turned empty, my zest for life departed.'

Tagore felt the presence of Kadambari Devi's spirit around him. About thirty years after Kadambari's death Tagore composed the *First Sorrow*.

I was walking along a path overgrown with grass, when suddenly I heard from someone behind, 'See if you know me?'

I turned round and looked at her and said, 'I cannot remember your name.'

She said, 'I am that first great Sorrow whom you met when you were young (twenty-five).'

Her eyes looked like a morning whose dew is still in the air.

I stood silent for some time till I said, 'Have you lost all the great burden of your tears?'

She smiled and said nothing. I felt that her tears had had time to learn the language of smiles.

I asked, 'Still, today you've kept with you that youth of mine when I was twenty-five?'

Said she, 'Here, just look, my garland.'

I could see, not a petal had fallen from the garland of that springtime back then.

I said, 'Mine has become completely withered, but my youth at twenty-five is still this day as fresh as ever, hanging there about your neck.'

Slowly, she took off that garland, placing it around my neck.

'Once you said,' she whispered, 'that you would cherish your grief for ever.' I blushed and said, 'Yes, but years have passed and I forget.'

She added, 'He who is the bridegroom of my inner thoughts, he had not forgotten. Since then, I've sat here secretly beneath the shadows. Accept me now.'

Then I took her hand in mine and said, 'But you have changed.'

'What was sorrow once has now become peace,' she said.

Tagore was known to have created various artworks influenced by his poems, writings and songs. The collegium wanted to comprehend and understand the above to see if they had found any reflection in the painting. The artwork in question also found mention in the Catalogue Raisonné prepared by Biswas one and half decades earlier. However, unlike others, this artwork was merely mentioned by name with a description obtained from some old archives. There was no photograph and it had been presumed lost. The collegium wanted to compare it to the description in the old archives and later with that in the Catalogue Raisonné.

Obviously, this was only the beginning and other aspects of visual analysis they would use involved looking at other artworks from the supposed period to compare similarities in style, creation of lines, brush movements and so on. It was also important to closely examine the canvas and the frame for clues regarding the period of production. After the visual analysis showed concurrence, the next step would be to perform a chemical analysis on the pigment to ensure its composition was in line with other works of Tagore from the period.

The members of the collegium began their work by examining the artwork for some easy giveaways: for example, Tagore had not been professionally trained and thus did not understand the rules of chiaroscuro, the play of light and dark in an artwork, with strong contrast to create dramatic effect. Similarly, Tagore always painted the open eyes of his subject brightly, with the contour of the face clearly standing out from the background. None of the above defects were visible in the artwork in front of them.

The collegium then examined the old archives where the piece had found mention. While there was no photograph, the artwork had been described in detail. The sad face, reflecting melancholia and death, the heavily veiled woman surrounded by darkness, shades of grey and black, subdued colours were all present there in the piece. A closer analysis of the painting revealed that the formation of lines and movement of the brush was similar to that found in other known works of Tagore from the time. Tagore was known to use broad, strong brush strokes in his work with a dense cross-hatching technique. Analysis of the signature revealed the name Rabindranath Tagore written in a continuous smooth line in Bengali towards the bottom left of the painting and dated in Bengali '21/1/39'.

The members of the collegium felt that if this artwork was a forgery, it was amongst the best they had ever come across. The creator was well versed in Tagore's technique and was a master artist in his own right. Also, he had great command over art history. Their analysis had so far not found any discrepancy in the artwork. The artwork exhibited the same style, was created in similar medium, colours and so on as other known pieces by Tagore.

An analysis of the frame and canvas revealed that it belonged to the years 1935–40 and was consistent with the time period. In fact, the formation of fine dust particles which had accumulated in the artwork were also studied closely and analysed for age. There was a growing consensus within the collegium that this was an original work done by the Grand Master himself.

The back of the painting revealed various stickers and marks of identification that documented its movement from one gallery to the other. The earliest of these stickers belonged to a small art gallery in Baroda and was dated from the mid-1960s. This gallery had closed a few decades ago; however, research had confirmed its existence in the early 1960s and 70s in the city. Thereafter the artwork had been purchased by various galleries that had confirmed their ownership of the same. In fact, the artwork had been showcased in a few exhibitions in the early 1980s and thereafter the trail had gone cold, only to resurface at the recently held auction almost three decades later. During this period, it had been held in the private collection of a well-known collector who had remained anonymous. There was no information available regarding how the artwork had come into the possession of the gallery at Baroda. There was no further information regarding who purchased the artwork or whether it was gifted, stolen or destroyed. Hence, the provenance was not complete with a gap of twenty-five years during which its fate remained a mystery.

The final step was pigment analysis. A small cross-section of the canvas was scraped at one corner to take out a small amount of pigment. This was tested for its ingredients and constitution. The result showed the use of vegetative colours, was a trademark of Tagore's paintings from this time period.

Art authentication was not an exact science. It depended on the analysis of various forms of data, which thereafter had to be comprehended and interpreted. The results were at best an opinion which in this particular case was pointing to the artwork being created by none other than Rabindranath Tagore. The collegium apprised Biswas of their findings but the final decision as chairman of the committee was his to make. A press conference was called to announce the findings the next day.

≈

Chapter 31

The Public Trial

Jay reached the venue half an hour before time. No sooner had he alighted from the car than he realised that he had made a big mistake. There were at least half a dozen television media personnel standing in the porch, testing their equipment. The moment they saw him, they rushed towards him like a pack of wolves towards a stranded deer, microphones in hand, cameras rolling. He pushed them aside with the regular byte of 'No Comment' as he rushed inside the seminar hall, hoping to get some reprieve.

But there was none, not immediately at least. The crowds had gathered to witness a public hanging and as was the case in the Victorian times, the passers-by far outnumbered the relatives and friends. The hall was packed to the brim, the art fraternity seemed to be in full attendance, which was expected, but so were the socialites. He lost his cool as a few of them moved towards him for the regular meet-and-greet ritual, the kiss in the air, as if they were catching up at an evening cocktail completely oblivious to their surroundings. He was in no mood to entertain them, he cursed a few who didn't get the message and looked through the rest.

'Leeches, that's what they are, blood-sucking leeches,' he cursed. 'They have little at stake, but look at them fill up the gallery.'

'Are these people for real,' he wondered?

He found a seat in the corner of the third row away from the limelight and the chatter. He sat down to analyse the gathering in the room. As he looked them in the eye, they nodded their heads in acknowledgement, some even sported a fake smile but he could see beyond the façade—they had blood in their eyes. A majority of them wanted him to be hanged.

He didn't blame them. Such was the norm of the society in which he lived, survival of the fittest. After all, who didn't enjoy a public hanging? The fall of a public stalwart, blood and flesh splattered across the room was great entertainment. The media wanted it, bad news was good for TRPs. The socialites hoped for it, it would provide the necessary masala for their gossip mills, at least for a few weeks till a new scandal happened.

Rumours were already floating that Jay Malhotra, the rainmaker of yesteryears, was in deep trouble. Vultures were hovering over him, waiting for an opportune moment to strike.

However, there were a few people who wished for his survival, hoping that he would pull a miracle, as he had done in the past. They did so not because they liked him or had an affinity for him, but because they knew that their destinies were interlinked. They were occupants of the same boat, invested heavily in the survival of the Navaratnas. The boat was unstable and sinking. They needed each other to survive, they needed every able hand to manoeuvre it to safety. Such moments didn't afford them the luxury of personal likes and dislikes. Jay was a lucky bastard, a survivor, who always sprung back from the brink of death. They prayed for their own sake that he would do so again.

Irrespective of the camp you belonged to, the anxiety and wait was killing. There was a strong undercurrent in the room and it seemed as if the place were going to explode.

Jay looked worried and disturbed, even a little unkempt, which was most unlike him. Gone was his customary self-composure and confidence. He scorned at a few print journalists who again tried to make polite conversation, hoping to get a few bytes for their story.

Unknown to anyone else, he had been trying desperately to reach Biswas for the past few days, hoping to shed light on the findings of the collegium but without any success. He must have called him a dozen times since yesterday, always reaching his voice mail. They had parted on a bad note the last time they had met. Biswas was eccentric while in the midst of his work, but he always returned his calls. This was the first time that he hadn't.

He felt vulnerable; his future depended on the findings of the collegium. And this was the reason why he had given the task to Biswas, whom he considered his dear friend and confidant. But he should have known better. It was his fault—he should have known that Biswas would never compromise his work; his integrity and work ethics were unquestionable.

He was stupid to think that Biswas would manipulate the process and bias the conclusion in his favour.

He cursed once again, 'Biswas is not at fault. I made a mistake, I should have gone to someone else.'

'If it wasn't for him, I wouldn't even have survived the auction,' he thought. 'He is perhaps the only person I can trust, my only friend and benefactor.'

Further, to add to his discomfort, Patel had become overly aggressive and abusive, filing a complaint with the Economic Offences Wing of the police. As a result, Jay had spent two long nights at the police station, trying to talk sense to them about art, provenance and authentication, only to realise that they didn't care. A person had filed a complaint and they were merely doing their job, asking questions. He had also tried unsuccessfully to talk sense into Patel, make him understand that he had merely been bidding on his behalf at the auction. The blame was not his to take, not entirely in any case. But his words had fallen on deaf ears, Patel was on a different trip altogether and had become more infuriated. He feared what Patel had in store for him and it was for this reason that he hadn't slept lately.

As he contemplated what he should do next, he saw Patty entering the seminar hall.

Oh my God! She was holding hands with Deepak Patel, who appeared to be her chaperone.

So this is why he has been acting difficult, he realised; the bitch must be fuelling the fire.

They sat down in the first row, in the midst of all the action. The tide had turned once again, the queen had retaken her throne and his future in contrast looked quite bleak.

After a few minutes, Patty left Patel's side and walked towards him.

'Jay! Are you all right?' she asked. 'You look miserable, my poor darling, unshaven and unkempt with dark circles under your eyes? Haven't been sleeping well lately, have you?'

'Stop playing games, Patty. Look around you, this is serious,' he replied.

'Oh, I know it is,' she said. 'Deepak is such a sweetheart; I wish you had introduced us earlier.'

Then moving closer to him, she whispered in his ears, 'He tells me that he will take you to the cleaners. But, don't worry, I wouldn't let him harm you, not yet at least.'

He was pleasantly surprised by her words. No, not the bit about Patel taking him to the cleaners, he quite suspected that. He was surprised that she didn't want him harmed. He didn't expect any help from her—she was the one who had raised the issue of provenance, and she was the reason for his current misfortune.

'Surprised?' she asked. 'I guess you still haven't figured it out.'

Now he was completely lost. 'What!' he yelled.

'Oh! You are such a fool' she said. 'You disappoint me, Jay Malhotra. All this time I thought I had found a worthy adversary in you. Weren't you surprised to see all those paintings at the auction, the Navaratnas? Didn't you wonder who the owner was? It seems to me that I had more confidence in your abilities than you did in yourself.'

As he mulled over her words, the first signs of anxiety

began to surface on his face.

'So, she didn't sell the entire lot of paintings to me. Obviously, she knew that I was acquiring them. She held on to them for over a decade, a period during which I increased their prices in multiplies. She must have more of them, that's why she doesn't want me harmed. But, the million-dollar question is how many more?'

As he looked up again, she was posting a wide smile, a smile of satisfaction.

'So, how many more paintings do you have?' he asked.

'Ah! Finally, you have caught on and you ask the right question,' she said. 'Well, the answer is enough, I have enough paintings to see you drown.'

'But, obviously, that's not what you want,' he said. 'Otherwise, we wouldn't be having this discussion.'

'Intelligent, you are,' she said. 'You will not sell a single painting from your inventory until all the paintings in my possession have been sold. If you agree, we can find an amicable solution.'

'And what do I get in return?' he asked.

'You will live to see another day,' she said.

'You don't give me much of a choice,' he said. 'But do get that monkey off my back.'

'Patel? I wouldn't worry about him,' she said. 'You concentrate on selling those paintings, I will manage Patel, make him dance around my fingers.'

As she got up to return to her seat, she again glanced at him.

'I will keep a close watch on you,' she said.

'I have no doubt,' he said. 'No doubt at all.'

'By the way, I am curious, is that painting authentic?' she asked.

'You should know, didn't you sell it?' he replied.

'Oh! No, not that one, I didn't.'

'I don't know the outcome.'

She looked at him disappointedly.

'I thought you were bum chums with Biswas and this was all a set-up.'

'In that case, all I can say is that you don't know Biswas well enough,' replied Jay sheepishly.

She returned to her seat without looking back at him.

Jay was a relieved man, he had just bought peace by selling his soul. He didn't care how many paintings she had in her possession, or for how long he would have to play her slave. What mattered was that he had managed to survive, live to see another day and explore the opportunities that it offered.

WTF

Biswas Mukherjee entered the seminar hall along with other members of his collegium. As he sat down in the first row, one of his colleagues went up to the dais to announce the flow of the discussion. They would first discuss the methodology and thereafter hand over the dais to Biswas to announce the results.

As the discussion commenced on the methodology, Biswas sat quietly in a pensive mood, reflecting on his past life. He was undoubtedly one of the most celebrated art experts in the country, enjoying an impeccable reputation in the art fraternity. His persona was larger than life and no one could question his undying devotion to the development of art in India; first as a scholar at Shantiniketan, then as a curator and finally, as an expert and authenticator.

The previous few months had been hectic. He remembered the day when Maya, Jay's secretary had called him frantically, 'We are doomed, sir,' she had said. But he knew otherwise, he knew that the paintings would sell. The auction house had been in contact with him—they wanted his opinion on a few paintings, and he could tell by the excitement in their voice that there was a demand. That was the day he realised that the art market was turning the tide and the good times were coming back. He had no time to waste and needed to act fast.

His thoughts were broken by the announcement to come on stage.

As he limped towards the stage, he had a glint in his eyes. He knew what was needed to be done.

'Ladies and gentleman, the collegium is unanimous in their findings. The portrait of the veiled woman presented to them for authentication is a creation of the Grand Master, Rabindranath Tagore,' he announced.

There was instantaneous clapping inside the room with some people rushing to congratulate Jay, who looked relieved that this chapter was finally over.

After the clapping had died down, Biswas continued...

'However, I beg to differ from their findings,' he announced. 'This is a masterpiece, I have no doubt, but not one created by Rabindranath Tagore.'

There was silence in the room as people looked up in astonishment.

Patty looked bewildered. She wondered who had delivered the anonymous note to her gallery regarding the incomplete provenance of the painting.

Jay looked perplexed. 'What is happening?' he wondered.

'My doubts were confirmed when I examined the sticker on the back of the painting belonging to that gallery in

Baroda,' announced Biswas. 'That summer afternoon almost five decades earlier is still fresh in my mind, as I was present there in person.'

He could feel the anger and frustration subsiding in his heart. For too long, the artist had lain hidden under the façade of the art expert. The time had come for the resurrection. The artist would live again...

As the audience grappled to absorb what he had just said, he yelled, 'I am the artist who created this masterpiece. Dozens of my creations adorn the walls of the leading art galleries and museums in the country. I am Arun, the artist you failed to recognise as the Master.'

There was complete pandemonium in the hall.

Patty realised that she had been taken for a ride as she pieced together the events of the past. 'He had spent those years at Shantiniketan as a research scholar to locate and document his forgeries. He thereafter implanted the idea of the re-emergence of the Navaratnas in my mind and manipulated me into aggregating them on one hand, while he simultaneously worked on the Catalogue Raisonné on the other. He needed the Catalogue to strengthen the documentation of his forgeries, give them the provenance they never had. No wonder he was upset when I abandoned the aggregation of the Navaratnas midway. It all makes sense now. That's why he asked me to involve Jay. He knew that I didn't have the money but Jay did. I can bet my house that it wasn't Jay who poached him from me, it was Biswas all along.

'But what the hell he is trying to achieve by announcing this now?' she wondered. And then it dawned on her. 'Son of a bitch,' she said. 'He left me that anonymous note on the incomplete provenance of the painting. He used me, he knew how I would react. Oh Patty, you have been such a fool. He knew that I would take Jay's pants down and Jay would rush to him for help. He wanted this gathering, this platform, but why?'

As she looked down at her phone, there was horror in her eyes. It showed a dozen missed calls from her largest clients. She turned her head backwards to look at the television cameras and yelled, 'Is this feed live?'

Her self-composure and etiquette gone, she roared like a lioness, 'Someone take the microphone from this bastard, he is trying to crash the markets. Call the cops, he has committed a huge fraud.'

Journalists climbed on top of each other to get a news byte for their gossip-hungry viewers. Nothing got more TRPs than a scam and a scam in the exclusive art industry was priceless.

Deepak Patel stood on his chair, towering above the others, yelling at top of his voice. 'This is a conspiracy! You bastards! I will see you all in court!' But his voice was lost in the mayhem that prevailed in the room.

Jay rushed to the stage and pulled the microphone away from Biswas. He dragged Biswas to a corner and yelled, 'You fool, do you realise what you have done? They will bury you, put you behind bars. There is too much money riding on this market, this is the end of you.'

Biswas smiled, 'I don't care what they do to me now. I have done what I had to do. You have to make sacrifices to bring about change. I am at peace with myself.'

'But don't you understand that the art market will crash?' asked Jay.

'I understand perfectly well, Jay,' he replied. 'Your art market is doomed. It had to crash. It had degenerated. You recognised not the craftsmanship of the artist but the signature on the canvas, everything was about money. Now there is hope, there will be a new beginning.'

'How could you do this, Biswas?' Jay cried.

This wasn't a question but a plea of desperation from a child who had just witnessed the world he knew crumbling before his eyes. Jay knew that the submarket of the Navaratnas would drag the entire art market into oblivion, nothing would survive the collateral damage. The art market as it existed today in India was finished.

'I am sorry it had to end this way,' Biswas replied. 'I genuinely liked you, your aggression, you were the perfect weapon in my arsenal. However, when I spoke to you before the auction, I realised how precarious your position was, how outstretched and weak you had become. At the same time, the results of the auction suggested that the tide was turning. I knew I didn't have time and had to act immediately.'

As the cops arrived, Jay handed Biswas over to them.

He climbed down the dais and sat in one corner of the room with his hands over his face. He was in shock and awe at the same time. He couldn't believe what had just transpired. He had been completely outmanoeuvred and manipulated. He had no inkling that with every action he was playing into the hands of Biswas, a mere weapon in his grand plan to seek revenge on the art industry.

Just when he thought that all was lost, he felt a comforting hand on his shoulder. He looked up—it was Patty. He held her hand tightly. They both needed each other now, more than ever before, as they walked out of the seminar hall into the uncertain future.

Acknowledgements

A debutant writer goes through an arduous journey of ups and downs. Every day, his self-belief and conviction are put to test.

To my family, if it wasn't for you, this novel would have never seen the light of the day. Thank you for standing by me and believing in me when I had myself lost all hope.

To my buddies, thank you for paying for my beers and listening patiently to my stories, no matter how boring they were.

Writers of fiction are not experts. As such they must depend on original works of others. I am truly fortunate to all authors and producers of original or derived works.

I would like to express my deep gratitude to my Publisher, Rupa for believing in my dream and walking the path with me.

Finally, to the countless individuals, who supported and encouraged me throughout this long and difficult journey, who shared their knowledge, stories and life experiences with me, a big thank you.

www.ingramcontent.com/pod-product-compliance
Lightning Source LLC
Chambersburg PA
CBHW060344030726
47497CB00003B/589